Return
to
Wonderland

Return
to
Wonderland

Stories inspired by
Lewis Carroll's Alice

MACMILLAN CHILDREN'S BOOKS

First published 2019 by Macmillan Children's Books
an imprint of Pan Macmillan
20 New Wharf Road, London N1 9RR
Associated companies throughout the world
www.panmacmillan.com

ISBN 978-1-5290-0603-2

1 3 5 7 9 8 6 4 2

A CIP catalogue record for this book is available from the British Library.

Typeset by Nigel Hazle
Printed and bound by CPI Group (UK) Ltd, Croydon CR0 4YY

Contents

Acorns, Biscuits and Treacle

by Peter Bunzl

Alice's Adventures in Wonderland *was among my favourite books as a kid. It influenced one of my first stories, written aged ten, about a boy stranded on a desert island who, like Alice, encounters multiple magical creatures before he's finally able to find his way home. My dad kept that early effort for years. When he returned it to me recently, I realised it contained similar themes to this tale: a shape-shifting hero, a dollop of magic and a handful of Lewis Carroll's characters, repurposed for a new adventure. My ten-year-old self would be so proud to see my forty-three-year-old self's short Wonderland story in print. I hope you enjoy 'Acorns, Biscuits and Treacle' as much as we do!*

Peter Bunzl

One morning, Pig woke to discover he had been turned into a real boy.

Of course, it wasn't obvious at first to Pig that he'd become a real boy because, in many ways, pigs and boys are quite similar. His body was still the same shade of pink it had always been, and he was still splattered in the same brown splotches of mud he rolled in every day to keep the hot sun from crackling his skin.

It was only when he tried to stand from where he'd laid his head, in a patch of shade beneath an old fig tree, that Pig first noticed something was amiss. For he found he could not get up on all fours in the usual way, as each of his joints had moved about on his body, and where his trotters used to be were two flat hands with long thin fingers that looked like – and Pig *hated* to use this word – *sausages*.

For a moment, Pig wondered if he was still dreaming.

In his last dream, he'd been sniffing around in his favourite oak grove, beneath a crescent moon as wide as the grinning Cheshire Cat, searching for acorns. Instead, he'd found an open tin of twelve delicious-looking iced biscuits, each with pink writing on that Pig couldn't read.

Naturally he'd snuffled the whole box.

Pig flexed his knuckles and found that his new fingers

were quite sensitive and moved easily. He could feel every lump and bump on the ground with them.

He put a hand up to his face and felt about to see if that had changed too.

It had.

His ears had got smaller and now stuck out from the sides of his head, and where they had previously been, on the very top of his bald patch, he now had a thick thatch of hair, scruffy as a hay stack.

Curiouser and curiouser.

Where his large flat nose had formerly sat, taking up all his view, he now found a meagre round blob. Though when he felt that new nose, it turned out to be as snub as the old one. Pig picked at the holes in it with a finger, and that felt good.

Pig looked down at his hind legs. They had grown longer and thicker and now ended in big flat rectangular lumps – feet with toes that wiggled when he concentrated on them. He found having toes a pleasant change from trotters. Somewhere, in a far-off memory, Pig had heard a children's nursery rhyme that called fingers and toes 'piggies'. It seemed an odd name for them.

Gradually he was acclimatizing to his new body. So much so that he thought he would try standing up.

He climbed slowly on to his two long legs and pushed himself off from the ground.

For a few seconds, he wobbled like a newborn runt; then his knees buckled under him, and his legs gave way, and he fell over backwards.

It hurt quite badly, and Pig decided that walking on two legs was going to be more difficult than he had imagined. As far as he could tell, standing up like a human just meant you had further to fall.

He tried again. This time, things went better as he remembered he had arms and threw them out to balance himself, placing one palm on the rough bark of the tree to keep upright.

Then he discovered he could hold on to a branch with his new grasp-y fingers, and that helped him stay on his feet even longer.

Pig looked at the ground far below and felt pretty pleased with himself. Now he was standing like a real human boy, he thought he might perhaps give walking a go.

He picked up one of his big flat feet, tipped himself forward, and promptly fell over again. Flat on his face.

It took Pig a good part of the morning to learn how to walk upright on his hind legs – or his only legs, really, since the other two were arms now. He didn't know if his progress was quick or not, but it felt an immensely long time to him. Walking like this, Pig began to feel more human. Now that he was human, he wondered if he should change his name.

The trouble was he *liked* the name Pig. A kindly sow had given it to him when she'd adopted him. Not that it was unique; it was what the herd called everyone. Everyone except the littlest hogs, whom they christened Piglet, Runt or Oinker.

Names hadn't mattered to Pig back then, but one day he'd wandered off and got separated from the herd and hadn't known how to call them back.

Perhaps he should refer to himself as Boy, now that he was one. Maybe he could combine both names, and put the second one after the first, like humans did: Pig Boy.

Yes. That sounded good.

In the back of Pig's mind, he vaguely recalled being human once before, a long time ago. A smaller, tiny human. That's where the nursery-rhyme memory had come from. He'd had a mother who'd sung it to him, roughly. She might even have called him Pig – he had a hazy remembrance of that too.

Pig thought these things as he walked along, and the

wind blew around his skin, giving him goose bumps and making him shiver with cold. This, he surmised, was probably the reason – or was the word *raisin*? – that humans wore clothes. He'd need an outfit anyway if he were to venture forth from the woods and not make everyone he encountered run away in shock at his muddy nakedness.

Pig wondered where he could possibly find clothes to fit him, since he lived deep in the wilds, far from any human settlements. But surely, he thought, if he just kept walking, chances were he'd eventually stumble across something that was good enough to wear.

Some time later, after Pig had been meandering aimlessly for a good few hours without a plan, he came upon a clearing in the woods.

In the centre of the clearing was a stone well. Beside it, Pig noticed a few items of clothing strewn about: a woollen shawl, a long coat, a dainty pair of shoes and a big floppy straw hat.

Next to these was a bucket on a rope fixed to a winch above the well.

Pig approached the bucket and was surprised to find it full of an unctuous amber-coloured liquid. He dipped a finger in and tasted it. Delicious! Sticky, sweet and syrupy, like . . . treacle.

Pig was so hungry by this point that he scooped up big handfuls of the treacle and ate it as fast as he could. Then, since he couldn't see anyone around to whom the clothes might belong, he crouched down beside them and began putting them on.

First, he tied the shawl around his waist like a skirt; next, he climbed into the long coat. It took him a while to figure out which way up it went and whether the long skinny bits were for arms or legs, but when he finally got it on right, he buttoned it closed over his chest.

Last, he put the straw hat on top of his head, over his straw-like hair. It turned out its floppy edges excelled at shading his new side-ears from the sun.

Pig considered trying on the shoes too, even though they looked a bit on the small side and were so black and shiny, they would probably make his feet look like trotters again. He was about to attempt to push his feet into them when he heard a shout.

'HELP!' three voices yelled, reverberating around him.

Pig realized they were coming from down the well.

He peered cautiously over its edge, and there – on a

ledge in the half-light, near the bottom of the well – were three well-dressed young ladies.

'Help us, please!' they cried again in unison.

For some reason, Pig understood them perfectly well. He opened his mouth to reply, but since he had never spoken words before only grunts came out.

'HGGOR GNRR,' he said, and wasn't even sure himself what that meant.

'Throw down the bucket,' the tallest of the three girls said. 'So we can climb out.'

'HHOORRHGGH,' Pig said, and he threw the bucket into the well, winching it down on the rope to the three girls below.

The girls argued for some time about who should be rescued first. Finally, it was decided that the lightest and smallest of them should go.

So the littlest girl, who looked about ten years old, got into the bucket and tugged twice on the rope, and Pig wound the winch handle and pulled her up.

'Thank heavens!' she cried when she finally reached the top. 'You saved our bacon!'

She climbed over the parapet and fell against the wall's sticky stone buttress. Pig thought she looked jolly odd up close, for she was covered from head to toe in treacle. It must, he concluded, be a treacle well.

'Ugh,' said the smallest girl with a shiver. 'I feel quite ill.'

She took a few deep breaths, and then, when she was fully recovered, looked seriously at Pig.

'You're wearing our clothes.'

'I found them on the ground,' Pig replied. 'They fit rather well.'

He put his hand to his mouth in shock for the words had come unbidden. He hadn't intended to answer the girl in her own language, just like that.

'So you *do* speak,' the smallest girl said. 'My name's Tillie. What's yours?'

'Pig,' said Pig, shortly. He left off the *Boy* part as he hadn't quite decided on that yet.

Tillie eyed him suspiciously. 'Pig's a queer sort of name, especially for a boy wearing girls' clothes.'

'And Tillie's a curious sort of name for a girl covered in treacle who lives down the bottom of a well,' Pig replied indignantly.

Tillie tried to wipe the offending treacle from the arms of her dress, but it only smeared into the material and made things worse. 'It's very uncivil to comment on another person's appearance,' she said. 'And, anyway, I think you may have misconstrued our situation. We do not *live* down the bottom of a well. We fell down it. We live, in fact, in a house on the edge of the woods. We were merely sent here by our mother to get some treacle for the treacle tarts she wanted to make for the Queen of Hearts's annual croquet party—'

Here she was interrupted by the other two girls, whom Pig had entirely forgotten about, and who were still waiting to be rescued from the well themselves.

'I say, up there – throw down the rope!' they demanded.

Tillie's eyes went wide with shock. 'Good heavens!' she exclaimed. 'My sisters! They slipped my mind! I do tend to be a tad loquacious when I get going.'

She stood up, and she and Pig lowered the bucket again, and together they hauled up the middle-sized sister.

The middle-sized sister turned out to be called Elsie.

Then the three of them hauled up the biggest sister, whose name was revealed to be Lacie.

All three sisters stood in a line in order of size and tried to brush the treacle off one another, but this only made them stickier. Pig saw that Elsie was missing her shawl, Lacie her hat, and Tillie her coat, and realized that he was sporting an item belonging to each of them.

When they finally noticed he was wearing their clothes,

the two other sisters looked taken aback. Nonetheless, they didn't ask for their things back.

Tillie picked up her shoes and tried to put them on, but immediately treacle began seeping out of their sides, so she tied the laces together and hung them round her neck.

She would walk barefoot through the forest like Pig, she decided.

'We should be off home,' said Lacie. 'Our mother will be wondering what's kept us.'

The three of them untied the treacle bucket from the rope and set off with it out of the clearing. As they walked, they took turns to carefully carry the bucket so no treacle slopped over the sides. Lacie did most of the carrying because she was the eldest, and because the other two proclaimed themselves thoroughly sick of treacle.

Pig went along with them since he had nowhere else in particular he had to be.

'Who is your mother?' he asked, following the three treacle-dripping girls along a narrow path through the woods that they were navigating with some familiarity.

'Why, she is the cook to the Duchess, of course,' said Tillie. 'The whole of Wonderland knows that.'

'The Duchess?' said Pig, for that name sounded familiar.

'Yes,' said Elsie. 'Three-hundred-and-sixty-six days ago,

the Duchess told our mother to bake some tarts for the Queen of Hearts so she could take them to her annual game of croquet.'

'So Mummy sent us out to get the treacle from the well,' Lacie continued, 'only . . . well, the three of us ate so much of it when we arrived that we got a touch overexcited and decided to have a Caucus race.'

'What's a Caucus Race?' Pig asked. He'd been gathering acorns from the side of the path and snuffling at them with his nose while they spoke. Even though he was a boy now, he couldn't help himself, for there were so many tasty-looking ones strewn about.

'A Caucus race is a race in a circle,' Elsie explained. 'In this case, round the well. It starts when you want to begin and finishes when you want to stop.'

'And while we were doing that,' Tillie added, continuing with the story, 'we each of us slipped on a separate patch of treacle and fell down the well.'

'We were hoping it might be the gateway to somewhere,' Elsie said. 'To another world that was a trifle less curious than this one. But, no – it just turned out to be a plain old treacle well.'

'So we were stuck down there for a year and a day, living on treacle, which is no better than trifle, really,' Lacie said.

'And with no one to rescue us. Until you came along.'

Pig gave a grunt of sympathy. 'I'm sorry to hear that,' he said.

'Where *do* you come from, exactly?' Elsie asked.

'And why do you act so funny?' Tillie added.

'I'm not entirely sure,' Pig replied. 'Last night, when I went to sleep beneath my favourite fig tree, I was a wild pig. I dreamed of eating a tin of biscuits in an oak grove . . . and this morning, when I woke, I had turned into a real boy. The funny thing is, now that I am a real boy, I recall being one before – a boy who was a lot . . . smaller. A tiny baby, in fact. As for why I act so funny, well . . . I'm trying my best to do boyish things, but the truth is I'm still slightly piggy inside.'

Pig told this whole tale quite fluently, and was mystified to find he had no trouble getting so many human words out. Once he had finished, he looked up to find that the four of them had arrived at the edge of the woods.

There, beyond the last few trees, behind a low picket fence, stood a cosy-looking cottage that looked awfully familiar, with ivy and roses winding round the door, and a thatched roof that was barely higher than he was.

On the cottage doorstep sat a Frog-Footman in a powdered periwig and a dress coat. He had his hands over his face and was sobbing profusely. 'Tillie, Lacie, Elsie!' he called out in surprise when he looked up and saw the three girls approaching. 'Do my sore eyes deceive me? How terribly late you are back for your supper! Tragically late!'

'Why?' Tillie asked. 'What's happened, Froggy, dear?'

'Countless awful things!' The Frog-Footman wiped his cheeks with a corner of his wig. 'Three days after you vanished, the Duchess gave her son – her baby boy – to a strange girl called Alice who was passing through, and he turned into a piglet right there in her arms, wiggled free and ran off into the woods! Afterwards, the Duchess declared she didn't care for such naughty babies. And the cook said she didn't either, not for the lost child, nor for the girl called Alice, nor for you, her own three missing daughters. Then the pair of them put on their glad rags and went off together to play croquet with the Queen of Hearts. The tournament went on for a week, and when they beat the Queen at her own game she shouted, "Off with their heads!" and it was done. I've been sitting here crying about it ever since.'

'How awful!' exclaimed Elsie.

Pig didn't know if she was referring to the fact that her mother and the Duchess had gone off gaily to play croquet despite their missing children, or the news that the pair of them had had their heads cut off, or the revelation that the Frog-Footman had been sitting on the front step crying for nearly a year and day.

'She was a terrible mother,' Elsie said.

'And a terrible cook,' Tillie added.

'She spoke most roughly to us and scolded us when we sneezed,' Lacie said. 'Which was relatively often, on account of the pepper she used on everything, even the laundry.'

'The Duchess was quite unpleasant too,' Elsie said. 'Remember the curses she threw at her baby. And the plates?'

'And what kind of woman gives her infant away to the first wandering stranger who passes through?' Tillie said.

'And to call her son Pig in the first place,' Lacie added. 'If that's not enough to set wild magic in motion, I don't know what is! No wonder he turned into a piglet!'

Suddenly, the three girls turned to Pig and stared at him.

'Didn't you say you used to be a pig before you were a boy?' Elsie asked.

'And didn't you also say that you recalled being a baby before that?' Lacie added.

Pig nodded.

'How did you get your name?' Tillie asked.

'Why,' Pig said, 'I thought the other wild pigs had given it to me. It's what they call almost everyone in the herd. But perhaps I've had my name from back when I was a human baby, in a kitchen filled with pepper and broken crockery. Yes, I recall now . . . the woman who nursed me did call me Pig. And there was someone else who was always smashing plates and making me cry rather loudly.'

'That was our rotten mother!' cried Tillie. 'And the rotten Duchess. You *are* her baby. We used to look after you. And now you're grown as big as I am – and in almost a year and a day too! However did you manage it?'

'Pigs grow a lot faster than humans,' Pig explained, although to him this felt as if it couldn't possibly be the reason. It was more likely the wondrous wild magic they'd referred to at work. He was only sad his mother wasn't there to see his triumphant return. However mean she'd been, he still dearly felt that he would've liked to have met her.

'But this means you're Duke!' Elsie said suddenly, for she was far more practical than the other two and consequently good at seeing what was what.

'Duke?' repeated Pig in shock.

'Yes,' said Lacie. 'And this is your new home.'

'Isn't it marvellous?' Tillie said. 'We live here too.'

Pig stared at the cosy and familiar little cottage with ivy and roses running up its walls, and a sudden sense of elation filled his heart until he felt he might soar as high as a hog on the wing.

He pushed past the Frog-Footman, who was now staring goggle-eyed at his new master, and reached out and opened the front door of the house.

Beyond it was a small kitchen full of smashed plates. It smelt so strongly and recognizably of pepper that Pig had to pinch his snub nose to stop himself from sneezing.

'Seems we're in charge now,' Lacie said, putting the bucket of treacle down on the table. 'Tillie, show Pig the Duke's old room so he can find something befitting to wear. Then get changed yourself. Elsie and Froggy and I shall start on the cleaning.'

Tillie took Pig to a grand room along the passage where there was a big old wardrobe filled with dusty clothes that had formerly belonged to the Duchess's husband, the Duke.

The Duke, Tillie explained, had gone out one day, thirty-three months ago, to play cribbage with the King, and when he'd beaten His Majesty by two whole lengths of the cribbage board, the monarch, who didn't like to lose at any game, especially not cards, had taken the Duke's head in revenge.

'Really, I don't know why anyone goes to play games with the monarchy,' Tillie said with a sad shake of her head.

The Duke, it seemed, had not been a pleasant man, and so it was no great loss to the dukedom. But the King was not a beloved ruler either, and neither was the Queen, which was just as unfortunate for the kingdom.

When Tillie finally left, Pig beat the dust from the Duke's old clothes and tried them on. He was pleased to find they suited him down to the ground.

Later, when he returned to the kitchen, he saw that Tillie, Lacie and Elsie had changed into clean outfits too and had done their best to tidy away the disorder. The Frog-Footman was nowhere to be seen, and Elsie revealed that he had rushed off immediately to tell the whole of Wonderland about the return of the new Duke.

Pig smiled at the three sisters, whom he'd rescued and who'd revealed to him the truth of who he was. He felt in his pocket for the handful of acorns he'd picked up on the way home and put them on the table.

'It looks like acorns and treacle for tea.' He sighed, for they were not the sort of things he imagined a duke should eat for dinner.

'If only we had something to go with them,' Elsie said.

'Oh, but we do!' Tillie dashed over to a footstool in the corner of the empty larder, reached up and pulled a biscuit tin from the very back of the top shelf.

Jumping down, she placed the tin in the centre of the table and took off its lid.

It was filled with the most delicious-looking biscuits, each piped with pink writing. And this time Pig could read exactly what the familiar words on them said:

'EAT ME.'

'Do you really think we ought?' Lacie asked.

Tillie shrugged. 'I don't see what possible harm it could do.'

The Queen of Hearts and the Unwritten Written Rule

by Pamela Butchart

I'm a big fan of all things weird and wonderful so Alice's Adventures in Wonderland *has always had a special place in my heart. My husband and I even had a Mad Hatter's tea party at our wedding – complete with cakes, a Mad Hatter Magician and one hundred tea cups full of Prosecco!*

I was delighted to be asked to be part of this wonderful collection of re-imaginings and of course chose to write about the wonderfully bad-tempered Queen of Hearts. I used to think a lot about this character as a child and found that as an adult I still had some questions about her. Does she have a softer side? Is she a necessary evil? Would she be any good at Parkour?

I had so much fun writing about what the Queen of Hearts has been up to since Alice left Wonderland and I really hope you enjoy reading it.

Pamela Butchart

OK. So, EVERYONE knows who Alice in Wonderland is and how she fell into a hole made by a GIANT rabbit and ended up in a place called WONDERLAND where everything was pretty weird.

But what loads of people DON'T know is what happened when Alice LEFT Wonderland. And what happened is that she forgot to SHUT THE DOOR behind her (but to be fair, that was probably because rabbit holes don't actually have doors, so it's quite hard to shut them).

So anyway, when Alice got back home, she started telling loads of people EXACTLY where the rabbit hole was and all about the TEA PARTIES and the QUEEN OF HEARTS and the rabbit who could TELL THE TIME. And it wasn't long before Alice got a bit famous, and then everyone wanted to go to Wonderland because it sounded BRILLIANT, and you didn't even need to buy a plane ticket or use your Oyster card or anything like that because rabbit holes are FREE.

So that's when people started abseiling down the rabbit hole for their holidays, and Wonderland got SO POPULAR that they even had to close Disneyland in Los Angeles AND the one in Paris because no one was going any more.

All the PEOPLE and ANIMALS and PLAYING CARDS that lived in Wonderland quite liked the fact that there were always loads of people on holiday in their land because when people go on holiday, they take SPENDING MONEY and then spend it all before they go home on stuff they don't even need, like T-SHIRTS with the name of the place they are in on it, and MAGNETS and TOBLERONES. And it wasn't long before everyone in Wonderland started opening SHOPS and STALLS selling all sorts of stuff like mini statues of Alice, and T-shirts with the Cheshire Cat's face on them, and ANTI-SICKNESS TABLETS (because some of the tourists got a bit travel-sick coming down the rabbit hole).

The Mad Hatter started hosting HUGE tea parties and making everyone pay for their TEA and MILK and SUGAR separately. And you even had to pay to RENT A SPOON to stir your tea.

So, anyway, everyone was loving having all the tourists in Wonderland, and the King of Hearts even declared that every Tuesday morning was ALICE MORNING and every Tuesday afternoon was ALICE AFTERNOON (with an hour break between them). And when the tourists asked why he didn't just make it ALICE DAY, he just laughed and said that they obviously didn't understand how Wonderland WORKS.

But everyone who lived in Wonderland knew that it was because the Queen of Hearts HATED Alice, and she didn't want it to be ALICE DAY when she was eating her LUNCH, because lunch was the Queen of Hearts's favourite meal, and she didn't want it being ruined every Tuesday. And she even said that she would probably throw up every last BIT of her lunch if she had to eat it on ALICE DAY. And no one wanted to see that, so the King of Hearts did the morning and afternoon thing instead.

All the tourists LOVED Alice, so the Queen of Hearts had to keep her hatred of Alice a SECRET from them, which was hard because the PALACE was one of the most popular places to visit in Wonderland, and it was even rated NUMBER ONE on TripAdvisor (which is a website people go on to complain about stuff they didn't like about their holidays, like if they found a hair in their food or if the sheets weren't white enough or if it rained).

So, the Queen of Hearts had to do loads of PRETEND SMILING when people came to visit. And one time she got so annoyed that she shouted, 'OFF WITH HIS HEAD!' while she was getting her photo taken with a small man who was dressed as Alice, and he almost got

DECAPITATED, and Wonderland ended up losing a WHOLE STAR on TripAdvisor because of it.

The Queen of Hearts didn't like the tourists much, and she DEFINITELY didn't like the CHANGES that were happening in Wonderland. But the King of Hearts said that he liked all the new YOUNG STUFF and that CHANGE WAS GOOD and also that they NEEDED THE MONEY. They probably needed the money because the King of Hearts liked being able to afford to buy every single type of cereal in the WORLD and eat it from a GOLD CEREAL BOWL and to be able to fly his PERSONALIZED HELICOPTER to the shops to get milk.

So the King said that the Queen of Hearts just had to GRIN AND BEAR IT, which meant that she had to fake smile and try not to scream, 'OFF WITH THEIR HEADS!' any more. And she found that really hard because chopping people's heads off was her favourite thing, and she liked it even more than she liked lunch.

But then one day someone went TOO FAR. And that someone was the Queen of Hearts's own DAUGHTER, because I forgot to tell you that after Alice left Wonderland, the King and Queen had a daughter, and they called her LITTLE QUEEN GERTALINE

WEETABIX CHEESE-AND-HAM SANDWICHES (but she just called herself Lil' Queen).

So, anyway, Lil' Queen loved how much Wonderland was changing because she was obsessed with NEW STUFF and TECHNOLOGY and SMOOTHIES, and she was always ordering people to come down the rabbit hole to set up new stuff in the palace. Like a little BUTTON she could press to make her bedroom curtains open and close, and a KARAOKE MACHINE, and those TOILET SEATS that are already WARM when you sit on them.

Even though Lil' Queen was only eight years old, most people in Wonderland were actually MORE scared of her than they were of the QUEEN of Hearts because she could shout EVEN LOUDER. And when she got annoyed she shouted, 'OFF WITH THEIR HAT!' (which might not sound nearly as bad as what the Queen shouted, unless you know that 'HAT' stands for 'HEAD, ARMS and TOES'!). So there you go.

Anyway, one morning, the Queen of Hearts went to check on her servants to see how they were getting on making her sandwiches. But when she stepped into the kitchen, she saw that her kitchen WASN'T a kitchen any more because it was a COFFEE SHOP.

The Queen of Hearts was FURIOUS about the

coffee shop replacing her kitchen because there was a giant COFFEE MACHINE where her SANDWICH COOKBOOKS used to be and about FIFTY people she didn't even know sitting around drinking coffee and asking her for the WIFI PASSWORD.

And she got even MORE furious when she saw that her husband was sitting drinking a cappuccino and watching FUNNY CAT VIDEOS on his brand-new laptop. EVERYONE knew that people in Wonderland were supposed to drink TEA, not coffee. So the Queen grabbed a piece of cake off someone's plate and starting eating it (because being furious made her really hungry). But then her eyes went REALLY WIDE, and she started spitting it out, because it was COFFEE CAKE – and that's when the Queen said that it was the FINAL STRAW and then she started pointing at everyone who was drinking coffee and shouting, 'OFF WITH THEIR HEADS!'

But before anyone had their head chopped off Lil' Queen came rushing in and said that it was OK because it was a POP-UP coffee shop, which meant that it could be folded back down and taken to a different part of the palace. But the Queen said that was WORSE because it meant that when she was walking around the garden, or putting her pyjamas on, or sitting on the toilet, the coffee shop might just pop up out of NOWHERE.

Then the Queen of Hearts said that coffee was now BANNED in Wonderland and that anyone caught drinking it or even SMELLING it would lose their head. She told Lil' Queen to get rid of all the new stuff she'd had installed in the palace, even the SMOOTHIE MACHINE.

As soon as the Queen said that about the SMOOTHIE MACHINE, Lil' Queen's face went RED. And then it went PURPLE.

And that's when Lil' Queen challenged her mum the Queen to a game of CROQUET, because even when the Queen of Hearts was in a terrible mood she still ALWAYS wanted to play croquet because she got to hit curled-up hedgehogs with FLAMINGOS, which she thought was brilliant.

Just before they started the game, Lil' Queen said that if SHE won then her mum had to let her keep her SMOOTHIE MACHINE, and that if the QUEEN won, she'd get rid of it and all the other stuff too, even the toilet seat that made your bum warm. When she said that, the King of Hearts looked down at the ground, and he looked a bit like he was going to cry, and it was obvious that he LOVED the toilet seat.

Everyone clapped and cheered as they watched the game, and someone even FAINTED when the Queen of Hearts won her first point. People took croquet very seriously in Wonderland, and they even had a Wonderland croquet WORLD CUP every four days, because four years was just too long to wait.

But then, just as the Queen of Hearts was about to win, the King of Hearts SQUEALED at a butterfly because he didn't like them, and the Queen of Hearts got such a fright that she dropped her flamingo, and it ran away. And that's when Lil' Queen cheered and said that she had WON the game of croquet and also that she had won COMPLETE POWER of Wonderland because of the UNWRITTEN WRITTEN RULE.

The Queen of Hearts just STARED at her because she had no idea what she was talking about. So that's when Lil' Queen called one of the guards to bring the CROQUET RULE BOOK and, when he did, Lil' Queen opened it and pointed to a blank page and said, 'SEE?' And the Queen said, 'I can't see anything.' And Lil' Queen said, 'EXACTLY.' And then she shut the book with a loud thump and explained that the UNWRITTEN WRITTEN RULE stated that if the Queen of Hearts ever dropped her flamingo while playing a game of croquet with her daughter then Wonderland would INSTANTLY belong to her daughter.

And EVERYONE gasped.

Then before the Queen of Hearts had a chance to say one word, Lil' Queen ordered the guards to take her away to a spa called 'CHILL' that she'd had made and said that her mum needed to stay there until she learned to be CALM and ACCEPT that Wonderland was changing. And that if she didn't she would be BANISHED from Wonderland for EIGHT WHOLE DAYS. And that's when everyone gasped again, because, even though eight days might not seem like a very long time, it meant that the Queen would miss TWO FULL CROQUET WORLD CUPS.

Even though the Queen of Hearts was probably the most furious she had ever been in her LIFE, she just went with the guards without trying to chop anyone's head off, because she didn't want to get BANISHED.

The Queen of Hearts hated the spa instantly because they made her wear a FLUFFY ROBE and get her FEET MASSAGED and there wasn't any normal tea with milk because there was only GREEN TEA. And when she got upset by things like people saying 'HELLO', all she wanted to do was scream, 'OFF WITH THEIR HEADS!' but she had to take a deep breath and not do that because she knew that the royal guards were watching her.

So the Queen of Hearts just sat on a yoga mat and pretended to look CALM and practised her PRETEND SMILING. But on the inside she was RAGING, and she knew she needed to come up with a PLAN to get control of Wonderland again.

Back at the palace, everyone was having a great time because Lil' Queen was getting LOADS of stuff delivered to Wonderland like COMPUTERS and LAWNMOWERS, and she'd even sent a smoothie machine to EVERY HOUSE in Wonderland and made sure there was one in every hotel room.

And then loads of POP-UP coffee shops started popping up everywhere, and there was a GIANT LIGHT-UP STATUE OF ALICE that you could go inside and then climb up a spiral staircase all the way to her eyes, where there was a SMOOTHIE BAR.

Even MORE tourists started coming to Wonderland, partly because they wanted to see all the new stuff, but also because Lil' Queen had installed an ESCALATOR in the rabbit hole so people didn't have to jump any more.

But then Lil' Queen said that she'd had ENOUGH of

croquet and that PARKOUR was the NEW CROQUET, and that's when people started to get a bit annoyed, because, like I said, people took croquet very seriously in Wonderland. And as soon as Lil' Queen saw that even ONE PERSON was a TEENY BIT annoyed about the whole Parkour thing she started screaming, 'HATS! HATS!' and so everyone just started running and jumping on and off stuff (because that's basically what Parkour is) because they didn't want to get their heads chopped off.

Back at 'CHILL', the Queen of Hearts was hiding in the toilets because someone outside was trying to make her drink an ENERGIZING BREAKFAST SMOOTHIE, and she absolutely hated smoothies because, like she'd told her daughter a hundred times, they were just TOO SMOOTH.

But then, all of a sudden, someone knocked on the cubical door, so the Queen pulled her feet up so that no one would know she was in there. And that's when someone wearing a bracelet that said 'YOLO' slipped a note under the cubical and ran away. And when the Queen of Hearts read the note she GASPED and then she GROWLED and then she KICKED THE DOOR DOWN WITH ONE FOOT, because the letter said:

*Lil' Queen lied to you. She made up the Unwritten
Written Rule (she wrote it herself and rubbed it out
just before the croquet match).*

Love from Your Biggest Fan

The Queen of Hearts had NO IDEA who'd slipped
the note under the door, but she knew exactly what she
needed to do. So she kicked off her FLUFFY SLIPPERS
and stormed RIGHT past the guards and out of 'CHILL'.
And when the guards tried to stop her she just gave them
a LOOK that obviously meant, *'I'm the REAL Queen of
Hearts. GOT IT?'* and they backed off.

The Queen of Hearts couldn't BELIEVE how many
tourists there were, and she had to cover her eyes because
of all the FLASHING CAMERAS and also because most
of them were dressed up like Alice. She ran through the
crowds – past all the pop-up coffee shops and smoothie bars
and a supermarket that only sold ORGANIC SEEDS –
all the way to the palace. And she must have shouted,
'OFF WITH THEIR HEADS!' about five hundred
times on her way (especially when she saw anyone with a
weird, twirly moustache, because those were new, and she
DEFINITELY didn't like them).

But when she got to the palace gates she saw that they

were locked. The CHESHIRE CAT was there, and so was the MAD HATTER and the CATERPILLAR and loads of other people, and they were all holding up SIGNS that said stuff like '*TEA FOR ME, PLEASE!*' and '*BRING BACK CROQUET!*' and '*SAY NO TO SMOOTHIES*'.

And that's when the Cheshire Cat came over to the Queen and said that he had something to tell her. So she asked what it was. And he asked HER what is was. And she asked HIM what it was. And it went on like that for ages until the Cheshire Cat EVENTUALLY told the Queen of Hearts that Wonderland was OUT OF CONTROL (and not the GOOD out of control that Wonderland usually was). And then everyone started going on about how there wasn't any GRASS left because of all the Parkour parks, and that the GOATS had started nibbling at everyone's ankles instead, and that there was actually only HALF A PACK of guards left.

And then the Caterpillar said that he was EXHAUSTED because all the coffee was making the Dormouse WILD and that he kept throwing MIDNIGHT dance parties and screaming into his new KARAOKE MACHINE.

The Mad Hatter said that he hadn't had a cup of tea in almost TWO DAYS because Lil' Queen had BANNED

TEA, and that's when the Queen of Hearts shouted, 'ENOUGH OF THIS MADNESS! OPEN THIS GATE!'

And when what was left of one of the guards opened the gate the Queen GASPED.

And it wasn't because of the giant light-up statue of Alice OR the hundreds of little Alice garden gnomes OR the new SUBWAY STATION next to the garden shed. It was because Lil' Queen had ripped up her CROQUET FIELD and replaced it with a CONCRETE Parkour park.

Well, the Queen of Hearts stormed RIGHT into the palace and up to her daughter's bedroom. But when she got there Lil' Queen was lying on her bed and she was CRYING because she said no one LIKED any of the new stuff, and that she'd got loads of letters from people COMPLAINING that they didn't like the SMOOTHIES because it didn't matter which fruit you used, they always ended up tasting like banana.

That's when the Queen of Hearts told Lil' Queen that she knew she'd faked the UNWRITTEN WRITTEN RULE and that SHE was back in charge. And then she said she hoped Lil' Queen understood now that it WASN'T EASY being in charge of a place like Wonderland and that she was sometimes a TEENY bit grumpy because it was hard work.

Lil' Queen nodded and said that she would never EVER try to take over Wonderland again. And then she asked if she was going to have her head chopped off, but the Queen said that she wasn't, but that she WAS grounded for FOUR WHOLE Croquet World Cups, and Lil' Queen was so upset that she screamed for SIXTEEN FULL MINUTES. But the Queen of Hearts just stood there and stared at her until she eventually stopped screaming. And then she said, 'Are you finished now?' And Lil' Queen said that she was.

So the Queen of Hearts went back out into Wonderland and started kicking down the pop-up coffee shops and pouring all the smoothies down the drain, and then she went into the ORGANIC SEED supermarket and told everyone to 'STOP EATING SEEDS, FOR GOODNESS' SAKE' and to eat a sandwich instead. And then she made them all bring EVERY SINGLE SEED that was in the supermarket and lay them down on top of the concrete Parkour park at the palace and water them until the grass grew back (which happened right away because it was Wonderland, and the grass actually grew so quickly that someone had to go and get the goats ten minutes after they'd watered the seeds).

The Queen of Hearts was DELIGHTED with the new

grass because it looked even better than the old grass, and she couldn't WAIT to play croquet.

That's when the King of Hearts appeared, and he had one of the TWIRLY MOUSTACHES and was wearing a knitted hat and jeans that were a bit too short and tight for him.

The King of Hearts looked a bit scared, and it was obvious that he was worried that the Queen was going to be MEGA ANGRY with him because he hadn't tried to do anything to stop Lil' Queen from taking over. But the Queen WASN'T angry with him. She just told him to go and make her a cheese-and-ham sandwich and to shave his moustache off IMMEDIATELY.

And then she smiled a TINY SMILE, and it was a real smile. And the King of Hearts smiled back. And they were smiling at each other because the Queen had spotted his 'YOLO' bracelet, and she knew that HE was the one who'd given her the NOTE and also that he was her BIGGEST FAN.

As soon as the Queen finished eating her sandwich, everyone CHEERED and said it was good to have her back (and they waited until she was definitely finished with her sandwich to cheer because they knew better than to interrupt her when she was having her lunch).

After that, the Queen put Wonderland back the way it used to be. Tourists were only allowed to come ONCE A WEEK so that they could visit the giant Alice statue, which she'd decided she liked because she was going to have the feet turned into CAKE so that she could look out of her window and watch Alice's feet get eaten every Tuesday.

And even though the Queen said that she didn't LIKE any of the new stuff, every night she would wait until people were in their beds, and then she'd sneak out and run around Wonderland doing PARKOUR. Because she thought it was BRILLIANT jumping on and off stuff, and actually she was quite good at it.

The Sensible Hatter

by Maz Evans

A chatty, silly show-off who likes to drink tea all day? It's hard to say what drew me to the Hatter! Wonderland is one of my earliest memories of a story transporting me to another realm as a bookworm child, and it is an immense privilege to spend some time here as a grown-up writer. Like the Hatter, I see the world in a slightly different way sometimes and not everyone sees it the way I do. My story is a chance to explore how the Hatter might be feeling inside, the side that perhaps his friends don't see. It's always good to step into someone else's shoes and try to look at the world from their point of view. If everyone did, there would be far less arguing and far more time to do very important things. Like drinking tea . . .

Maz Evans

'Anyone for gravy?'

The Hatter held his teapot aloft and watched his guests groan into their daffodil sandwiches. His heart sank. He just didn't understand it.

Every day at six o'clock, he would throw a really fun tea party. He always had a great time, but lately the Hatter had started to feel that no one else was enjoying themselves quite as much as he was.

He looked around his tea table. The Dodo spat out the armchair quiche. The Mock Turtle turned up his snout at the sausage scones. And none of the playing cards were eating the cupcakes – even though they were made from real cups. This was a fantabulous tea party. He'd even taken away the chairs to make it less boring. What was he doing wrong?

'I've got a splendaricious idea! Let's sing a song!' he cried. 'How about "Ring a Ring o' Noses"?'

'No,' said Bill the Lizard with a sigh.

'OK . . . "Baa Baa Black Ferret"?'

'Not again,' grumbled the Gryphon.

'"Old MacDonald Had a Cheesecake"?'

'MAY B L8R,' the Caterpillar spelled out with his smoke.

'Hey – what did we say about smoking at the table?'

The March Hare coughed as he poured another cup of sweetcorn juice.

'It's a vape,' huffed the Caterpillar. 'I'm trying to quit—'

The alarm clock in the jelly rang, signalling that teatime was at an end. Everyone started to hurry away.

'Same time tomorrow?' the Hatter called after his Wonderland friends.

'Oh, er, tomorrow?' said the White Rabbit, looking at his watch upside down. 'I really have to . . . wash my fur.'

'I can't make it either,' the Mock Turtle hastily declared. 'I have to . . . water my garden.'

'But – you live in a pond,' said the Hatter.

'Um . . . precisely!' said the Mock Turtle. 'Imagine if it ran out of water!'

'I can't make it for the rest of the week,' said the Cheshire Cat's head. 'I really must go to the dental hygienist.'

'All right,' said the Hatter sadly. 'I'll see you, then, Caterpillar.'

'NO,' the Caterpillar exhaled simply. 'GOT 2 GO.'

'Oh. OK,' said the Hatter quietly as everyone raced off. 'Well, have a wondoodleful day!'

But everyone had already left.

'What am I doing wrong?' he asked the March Hare as

he put his feet up on the dirty dishes. He hated cleaning up. It just wasn't tremenderful.

'Nothing,' said the March Hare, tipping the sleeping Dormouse out of the teapot. 'I think they were very rude. If they don't appreciate your hospitality, that's their problem, not yours.'

'Well . . . not *everyone* said they weren't coming,' the Hatter mused aloud.

'Er . . . they sort of did . . .' the March Hare whispered.

'So tomorrow, I'll just have to . . . throw the best tea party EVER!' said the Hatter. 'Now where's my recipe for welly-boot jam . . . ?'

At six twenty-two the following day, the Hatter and the March Hare were sitting alone at the table. The Hatter dipped his watch in the teapot to check it was working.

'How strange,' he said. 'I wonder where everyone is?'

The Dormouse, who had been woken up by the watch landing on his head, yawned. 'Aardvarks,' he said.

'Let's just enjoy our tea,' said the March Hare. 'These dandelion biscuits look lovely . . .'

A peal of laughter from the other side of the wood caught the Hatter's ear. Whatever it was sounded more fun than sitting at a nearly empty tea table.

'Back in a minutsicle,' he said, leaving the March Hare shaking his head behind him.

The Hatter hopped his way through the trees – he often hopped so that he didn't wear both his shoes out. The noise was getting louder – it was coming from the White Rabbit's house, just around the next corner . . .

As he arrived, he couldn't comprehend the scene that greeted him. But, as his eyes adjusted, he realized that they weren't deceiving him at all.

It was *another* tea party. And everyone in Wonderland was there.

He surveyed the tea table. There were cups of hot tea, finger sandwiches, pretty cakes and biscuits . . . It looked so *boring*. Why would anyone want to eat that?

'Um – hi, everyone!' he called over the happy hubbub, bringing it to an embarrassed hush. 'I thought you were all busy this evening.'

A guilty murmuring came in response.

'Look,' said the White Rabbit eventually, 'it's not that your parties aren't . . . interesting. It's just we all felt that if we were going to go to a tea party, we'd all like . . . well . . . some actual tea—'

'I do serve actual tea!' interrupted the Hatter defensively.

'With croutons floating in it,' whispered Tweedledum.

'Or in an upside-down cup,' said Tweedledee.

'Or not at all if it's the fourth of May,' grumbled the Gryphon.

'Well, who wants tea on the fourth of May?' scoffed the Hatter.

'WE DO!' everyone shouted.

'Your parties are just a bit . . . silly,' the White Rabbit declared. 'Would it hurt to be a bit more . . . sensible?'

'Sensible?' the Hatter repeated. He'd never thought of that before. 'Well . . . I suppose—'

'Super! That's sorted, then!' said the Cheshire Cat's grin. 'See you at six o'clock tomorrow.'

'Great,' mumbled the Hatter as he hopped sadly back through the woods. *Sensible*, he thought. He had no idea how to be sensible. Sensible was . . . well, it was just too . . . sensible. It really wasn't him. He couldn't help being silly. It was like a condition—

Suddenly, inspiration struck. Maybe that was the problem! He needed to find a cure for his silliness if he was to become sensible. And if he wanted a cure there was only one person who could help him.

'So how can I help you?' asked Dr Liddell, the Wonderland Doctor, early the following morning. 'You haven't been eating oysters with the Walrus and the Carpenter, have you? They've had food poisoning for days . . . Or have you been running in the Caucus race? I keep telling them – if they won't warm up, they will pull hamstrings . . .'

'No, no – nothing like that,' said the Hatter, balancing his hat on the end of his big toe. 'I need to be more sensible. I need you to cure my silliness.'

'Ah – the Sillies.' The Doctor smiled. 'There's a lot of that about.'

'Can you cure me?' asked the Hatter.

'Being silly isn't something to be cured,' the Doctor said. 'It's part of who you are.'

'But what if I don't want to be silly any more?' asked the Hatter.

'Well, that's a different matter,' said the Doctor. 'Perhaps you can choose not to be silly. Although, are you sure you want to?'

'Yes!' cried the Hatter. 'All of my friends think I'm too silly. If I change, they'll come to my tea parties again.'

'A friend who wants you to be someone else isn't really friends with you,' said the doctor.

'But I want to be sensible,' pleaded the Hatter. 'Please.'

Dr Liddell gave him a long, hard look.

'I'll tell you what I'm going to do,' he said eventually,

reaching into his cupboard. 'I'm going to give you two medicines.'

Dr Liddell pulled out two items. One was a pink cake with EAT ME written in currants across the top. The other was a small orange bottle, which had the words DRINK ME printed in green letters on its label.

'The first,' Dr Liddell told the Hatter, 'will make you sensible. But, if you don't like it, the second will change you back. I'll leave the choice entirely to you.'

The Hatter gratefully took the first and read the instructions on the label.

'*Take two nibbles of EAT ME at four-hourly intervals to cure the Sillies*,' he read aloud. '*Warning: possible side effects include sound financial planning and practical footwear.*'

'Two spoonfuls of this DRINK ME will reverse all the effects if you so choose,' the doctor told him, handing the second medicine over.

'Thanks, Doctor!' said the Hatter, springing up from his seat.

'My pleasure,' said the Doctor. 'One way or another, I hope you feel better soon.'

But the Hatter was already hopping out of the door.

The moment he was outside the Doctor's surgery, the

Hatter looked at the two remedies in his hands. He stuffed the bottle in his cardigan pocket.

'Won't be needing that,' he said under his breath – and instead took two nibbles of the cake. He shut his eyes and waited to be sensible.

Nothing happened.

The Hatter stood there for he didn't know how long with his eyes scrunched tight, but he felt no different whatsoever.

He opened his eyes and let out a big sigh. How very disappointing. He had so hoped that the Doctor would cure him. He started to hop home.

'Actually,' he muttered to himself, 'hopping is a highly inefficient way of moving around. And it doesn't actually save my shoes, as I hop on both feet equally. A brisk walk would make more sense. It's excellent cardiovascular exercise while making fewer demands on my muscles.'

The Hatter walked home carefully. He looked up at the trees lining his route. The weather must have changed since he went to the Doctor – everything seemed rather . . . grey. Usually he enjoyed wiping the tears of a weeping willow or spreading jam on the breadfruit trees. But, now he knew he'd never be sensible, that all just seemed a bit silly. Perhaps he'd come back and plant some nice plain fir trees. Why would anyone want gum trees blowing big pink bubbles at them?

The Hatter loosened his yellow necktie. Now he thought about it, a long coat and tie were impractical choices for the spring, when the weather was statistically likely to be fair. And a top hat was rather overdressed for a weekday – in fact, upon reflection, it was a silly item of clothing to wear every day. Perhaps he should take it back to the shop? Thank goodness he'd had the good sense to keep the receipt. Besides, a shopping trip might cheer him up. Yes, he might never be sensible, but at least he could dress more practically for daily life. He walked up to the crossroads, ignoring a catkin trying to purr at him on the way, and headed for the Wonderland clothing shop.

'Wow – what happened to you?' said the March Hare as the Hatter walked through his front door.

'Nothing much,' said the Hatter. 'I just thought I'd buy some new clothes. My others were silly.'

'If you say so,' said the March Hare, looking at him curiously. 'I liked them. And . . . a *brown cardigan*?'

'It's a sound choice for this climate,' said the Hatter. 'Paired with this beige shirt, I have the option of its warmth, or I can discard it in pleasant weather.'

'Where's your hat?' asked the March Hare.

'I exchanged it for these sturdy walking shoes,' said the Hatter, demonstrating the solid brown footwear. 'These will make my thirty minutes of daily exercise much easier.'

'I see,' said the March Hare. 'Hatter, I—'

'And that's another thing,' the Hatter interrupted. 'I've been thinking about my name. It feels silly to be called by my job – after all, who is named after a description of themselves?'

'Er . . . the Cheshire Cat, the Caterpillar, the Queen of Hearts, the White Rabbit, all the cards, me . . .'

'No – it doesn't make sense,' the Hatter insisted. 'So I have decided to take a new name.'

'Great – how exciting!' cried the March Hare. 'What shall we call you? How about . . . Orion? Or Zanzibar? Or Lutwidge?'

'Gordon,' stated the Hatter. 'I would henceforth like to be known as Gordon.'

'Right.' The March Hare sighed. 'If you say so . . . Gordon.'

'Good.' Gordon nodded. 'Now, how are preparations for this evening's function going?'

'All under control,' the March Hare said with a grin. 'I've just brewed a big batch of cushion juice, the Bolognese tarts are rising beautifully and, as for the marshmallow soufflé, it's just sublime, if I do say so myself . . .'

'No, no, no!' cried Gordon. 'This won't do at all! This isn't what our friends want! Here – I've created a plan for tonight's tea party.'

He handed a neat file over to the March Hare and awaited his impressed reaction.

'Are you sure?' said the Hare uncertainly. 'This is all very . . .'

'. . . Sensible!' said Gordon, smiling. 'So let's get on with it.'

At six o'clock precisely, the guests arrived in the garden, looking around uncertainly.

'Welcome,' said Gordon, who had considered changing for the party, but soon realized he'd risk staining his new clothes. 'Please, everyone, take a seat.'

'There are seats?' muttered the Gryphon, charging towards the table. 'Out of my way before he moves them.'

'No, no – each individual has an allocated place, denoted by their name card,' said Gordon. 'I have arranged everyone alphabetically.'

'Makes sense,' said the White Rabbit, hopping to the end of the table.

'So what's for tea?' said the Cheshire Cat's grin.

'I have selected a menu that will meet everyone's nutritional needs and avoid any allergies, food intolerances or too much saturated fat,' said Gordon, as the March Hare placed a small plate of celery in front of each guest. 'There is also significant scientific evidence that small, regular meals are better for one's metabolism.'

'What's for pudding?' asked the Dodo, eyeing his large celery stick unenthusiastically.

'Our diet is too full of refined sugar,' Gordon announced. 'I thought it sensible to skip dessert in favour of a twenty-minute stroll to aid digestion.'

'Oh . . . OK,' said Dormouse through a yawn. 'Can we at least have some tea?'

Gordon tutted. 'My research into the side effects of caffeine made terrifying reading. In fact, when I stopped to think about most drinks, they all have sizeable drawbacks. So here you go . . .'

He poured the contents of his teapot into everyone's cups.

'H_2O?' spelled the Caterpillar with his smoke.

'Trust me,' said Gordon, nodding sagely. 'Water is the most sensible choice.'

'So . . . we've come for a tea party, and you're feeding

us celery sticks and water?' the White Rabbit said slowly.

'That is correct,' Gordon confirmed. 'And while you are partaking, I look forward to a vigorous debate about Wonderland's politics. I have serious concerns over the Queen of Hearts's justice system . . .'

Gordon saw his guests exchanging uncomfortable looks. He didn't understand – this was exactly what they had wanted – a sensible tea party.

'Um . . . Hatter . . . ?' the White Rabbit began.

'It's Gordon.'

'Sorry . . . Gordon,' the White Rabbit continued. 'Are you feeling all right? You don't seem entirely . . . yourself.'

'I am very well, thank you,' said Gordon. 'Never better, in fact. By the way, who is free to help me clear out my loft this weekend? Senseless keeping all that clutter when the space would be ideal for a home office . . .'

'I see,' said the Cheshire Cat, who wasn't smiling for once. 'Aren't you going to spend your weekend painting pencils? Or washing the grass? Or playing the saucepan?'

'No,' said Gordon. 'Those things are . . . silly. There are more sensible ways to spend my time.'

'R U SURE?' the Caterpillar puffed.

'Utterly,' said Gordon, pulling the DRINK ME bottle from his cardigan pocket. 'In fact, I don't even know why

I'm keeping this. The doctor said it would reverse the effects of the EAT ME cake I took to cure the Sillies, but, as that hasn't done anything, I'm just going to throw this so-called "antidote" away . . .'

'NOOOOOOOOOO!' cried all his guests together.

'Why don't you, er, give it to me?' said the March Hare, prising it from his fingers. 'I'll throw it away for you.'

'All right,' said Gordon. 'But make sure you recycle the bottle. Far too much refuse ends up as landfill in Wonderland. It's a senseless waste.'

'I know just what to do with it,' said the March Hare, looking around the other guests. 'Leave it with me.'

'Excellent,' said Gordon, picking up a celery stick. 'Now who has any top tips for bathroom grouting? No sense in having messy tiles . . .'

An hour later, Gordon was tidying up the cups and plates – it made sense to do it straight away or it would be just another job for the next day – when the March Hare approached.

'Here,' said the March Hare. 'A present from your friends to say thank you for the party.'

Gordon was not displeased about this. A present meant they must have enjoyed his event. That just made sense.

Gordon reached for the bottle and read the label.

'A vitamin-filled, zero sugar, caffeine-free health drink proven to bring out the best in you. So DRINK ME.'

Gordon considered this carefully. He knew it was important not to eat or drink anything if you didn't know what it was. But, then again, it was a present from his friends. They wouldn't do anything to hurt him. There was no sense in it going to waste, especially if it was going to do him good. And, in any case, all that walking had made him thirsty.

Gordon opened the bottle and, seeing the March Hare's encouraging smile, drank down the contents.

The liquid tasted of cherry tart, custard, pineapple, roast turkey, toffee and hot buttered toast. It was like drinking a liquid smile. Immediately, he felt happier and brighter and – well, back to his old self.

'Gordon,' said the March Hare. 'How do you feel?'

'Superlicious!' he cried 'I feel fabbydoodles! Perfectuous! Tremenderzing! And now I think about it, *Gordon* is rather dull. I prefer the Hatter!'

The March Hare laughed. 'So does everyone else.'

'Now tell me,' said the Hatter, yanking off his cardigan and using it to wipe the plates. 'What's for tea?'

*

Everyone in Wonderland agreed – it was the best tea party ever. The sardine cookies were a triumph, the cornflake pie was sublime, and the aubergine milk went down a treat.

'It's so good to have you back, Hatter,' said the Dodo, chewing happily on a fondant fishcake. 'Wonderland just isn't nearly so . . . wonderful without you.'

The Hatter smiled and tapped his hat. Perhaps the Sillies weren't so bad after all.

'Anyone want a drink?' he said, holding up his teapot.

The White Rabbit laughed. 'Go on, then,' he said. 'It's not gravy, is it?'

'Of course not!' said the Hatter, filling the rabbit's cup to the brim. 'We don't have gravy on Wednesdays! That would be ridiculous!'

The White Rabbit looked down at his cup with a smile.

'On Wednesdays,' said the Hatter with a wink, 'we have custard . . .'

The Missing Book

by Swapna Haddow

I first came across Carroll's Wonderland when I watched the Disney animation as a child. The nonsense of it all had me gripped and it wasn't too long after that I went hunting for Alice's Adventures in Wonderland *in my local library. I borrowed it so many times on my sister's library card that I'm still paying her back for the fines!*

When I was approached about the Return to Wonderland *anthology, I was honoured to be able to play with this timeless classic. I felt immediately drawn to the Mock Turtle. I love how self-absorbed he is. Arrogant characters are so much fun to write. His passion for learning immediately inspired a story about a library. This was my chance to write an ode to all the librarians who encouraged my love of reading and took me to wondrous worlds between the pages, including Wonderland itself.*

Swapna Haddow

A book, you must understand, can be a terrible thing. The most terrible of terrible things. Books, you see, are full of stories. They sit on shelves, maybe on floors, perhaps even on desks and tables. They are sometimes large, sometimes wide, sometimes slim, sometimes creased. But all of them sit. Sitting there, unassuming and waiting.

And what sits in wait can be quite terrible.

Which is why you need a librarian.

A librarian is a guide. They navigate the treacherous oceans of words and sentences and steer you clear of all these terrible things.

I happen to be a most marvellous librarian. You see, I am the most knowledgeable of all the Wonderland residents. I've had the finest of educations and, quite honestly, if you met some of the other Wonderland creatures, I'm sure you'd agree that they are dafter than a fish without a porpoise.

This was never more evident than when I met a girl with yellow hair and a blue dress at the beach. Her name was Alice. She told me about her adventures in Wonderland, and I, in turn, told her about my life. Alice had never met a Mock Turtle, and I think I came as quite a shock to the dear girl, who had never encountered a shelled creature of such intellect.

As we spoke – and thankfully it was mainly I who spoke, and she who listened, since she didn't have much of a head for information or for sticking to the point – she reminded me that everyone, even girls with yellow hair and blue dresses, deserved to have the most basic of knowledge, though they may never reach the distinguished level of a mock turtle, like me.

And so I took it upon myself to set up Wonderland's first library: the Library for the Curiouser and Curiouser.

Luckily for you, I shall be your guide for the course of this story.

Now, come along, because we have a mystery to solve.

I was sorting through the books in the library one day, counting them and checking they were all in their places. There are seven in total. That's all any library needs. The Gryphon, a regular library user, once commented that this was highly illogical, and I shall tell you what I told him: *'Never forget, dear Gryphon, that there are stories within stories, and even more within those, which is why seven books is quite enough. Any more, and it's impossible to keep control of the chattering and prattling of the words, particularly the rhymes.'*

It's very important that a library only stocks obedient books. Obedience is key. A book that misbehaves can easily turn the others, and suddenly there is a rampage of illustrations and sentences, causing havoc and challenging us all. That simply won't do.

Occasionally you find a library packed to the high ceilings with stacks of books, the weight of which bends the walls and cracks the floor. Stories shouting louder and louder to be heard, prancing about the place, leaving their mark. It's utter chaos.

That's why there are only seven books in my library. One mystery story, of course. And then six more. If you count them up, that's seven in total.

Which is why as I counted the books I was horrified to see a book on the Missing Book shelf. A book that did not tally.

I counted the books again. One, two, three, four, five, six and seven. And another one on the Missing Book shelf.

Again, I counted.

Again, seven in their place, and one in the dark, cavernous shelf that was always empty.

A book on the Missing Book shelf meant only one thing: a missing book.

A *missing* book!

A *MISSING* book!

How could this have happened?

I looked around my library. All of it seemed in order, as it always was. The book of woeful tales next to the book full of comedies so it could cheer itself up. The book full of facts sitting happily by the children's book in the adult section, because adults are always losing sight of their youth, and that's a fact. And, of course, the dog-eared book was as far as it possibly could be from the book about cats, but near the book about sticks, which was on the opposite side from the book about unsticking, to avoid confusion – you see?

Everything was exactly as it should be and in its place, as any good librarian would confirm.

This could mean only one thing: a horrible crime had occurred, and *I* had to solve it.

Being very fluent in solving mysteries, thanks to my fine education, I had my suspicions. But when unravelling clues it is important to be logical and to collect evidence. You must not reveal your suspicions too early, just in case you are wrong – and I never like to be wrong.

I thought back through the previous day. When one solves a mystery, it's important to retrace the events that led to the mystery. And then to use what you have discovered to solve that mystery towards which we have been retracing our steps.

* I'd seen the Gryphon first. He'd come in as he always did to sing and distract me from my librarian duties
* Next to come to the library was the Frog-Footman. He needed to deliver an invitation from the Duchess
* He was closely followed by the Dormouse, who wasn't here long at all
* Finally, the Pigeon visited, because it's not a story without a pigeon

The Gryphon was a beast of a creature, who I often feared would damage my books as he unfurled his feathered wings and waved his long, heavy tail about. He had, as he always did, mistakenly visited the beach to look for me, before arriving at the library to tell me he'd forgotten I was no longer *on* the beach. And then, as he always did, suggested that perhaps the library should move to the beach so it would be closer to the sea.

'What a silly idea,' I'd said angrily. 'That would make no sense at all. No *good* library should have any books with words starting with the "C".'

Of course, he apologized profusely, and we got to talking about our yellow-haired friend Alice.

'Alice was a sweet girl, but she could never have been a librarian,' I said to the Gryphon, who was rather soft on the girl. 'Though her adventures in Wonderland would have made a good story. I would've stocked a book like that here.'

The Gryphon nodded. It's hard for him to agree that I'm right, due to his problematic arrogance, so I appreciated his nod. 'You're right, Mock Turtle,' he said. 'I do miss the stories she told about her escapades.'

'If you want to read adventures, you've come to the right place,' I replied.

I pointed out two stories: an addition story and a venture story.

The Gryphon had looked at me, confused. I remembered the look because it made him look rather cross-eyed, and I thought I might have a book to correct that too.

'What am I to do with these?' He took the hefty tome full of essays on ventures and exploits. 'I'm looking for adventures.'

'That's why you need the book on addition too,' I said, handing him the maths book. 'A venture without the "add" is simply just a venture.'

His eyes lit up, finally understanding. Do you see what I mean about the Wonderland residents being simple folk? They really are lucky to have me and my library.

We bade each other goodbye, and I got back to arranging my books.

It is clear that the Gryphon had nothing to do with the missing book.

The morning had been quiet after the Gryphon left, as it often is in Wonderland. I had busied myself by singing a song that left me quite emotional, and then I had busied myself drying my tears, which left me quite tired.

I must have dozed off, as most librarians can expertly do, before I was awoken by the Frog-Footman, in his full livery, bursting through the library doors.

He barrelled in, as he *always* did, never bothering to knock, and thrust an invitation on my desk, which I thought to be rather rude, considering a moment before I had been resting my tired head there. If you have ever been struck on the head with an invitation, you'll know this to be a most painful thing.

'For the Mock Turtle,' he announced. 'An invitation from the Duchess to dinner.'

I like invitations, so I decided to forgive the intrusion.

Then I remembered what a hideous human the Duchess was, so I went back to resenting the appearance of the Frog-Footman at my desk. He repeated the exact same message, as he *always* did, with only the slightest of difference in the order of the words.

'From the Duchess. An invitation to dinner for the Mock Turtle.'

'I heard you,' I replied, annoyed.

Having made his announcement twice, he observed me, the eyeballs of those eyes that sit far too high upon his head, rolling about the sockets as he watched me go about my duties in the library. I needed time to find a way to decline the invitation. The cook at the Duchess's house was a bit of a brute with the peppermill, and I had never liked the way she looked at me whenever she mentioned wanting to perfect her Mock Turtle-soup recipe. In my opinion, it is rather uncouth to talk of recipes that your guests could feature in.

'I await your reply,' the Frog-Footman said. 'I will stay.'

He sat down, and I didn't doubt for a moment that he would happily wait all day for my answer.

'Shall I sit here?' he asked, having already sat down without my permission. 'I can sit here for however long it takes.'

His inane chatter was giving me a headache, so I was rather pleased to see a small squirrel-like creature scuttle into the library when it did.

'I'm afraid I won't be able to attend dinner with the Duchess. I'm far too busy with the library,' I blurted out, quite pleased that I had found the perfect excuse. 'I bid you goodbye, Footman, as I must tend to the Dormouse now.'

The Frog-Footman pounded out of the library, almost squashing the Dormouse into a dormouse-patty, which I would've been most upset about, since trampled-dormouse does have the unfortunate habit of staining the floor.

It had been some time since I had seen the Dormouse. He rarely leaves his residence at the Mad Hatter's tea-party table.

'Dormouse!' I exclaimed. 'How can I help you, my little friend?'

The Dormouse looked around the library to make sure he wasn't about to be trodden on before clearing his throat.

'I'm looking for a book on tea,' he said. 'Specifically tea parties.'

'I have seven books here,' I said. 'I know just the book for you.'

'If you just point me in the direction of the "T" aisle, I

am sure I can find what I'm looking for,' he said hurriedly.

'That won't do, Dormouse. Books can be a terrible thing without proper guidance,' I explained. 'You see, the "T" books contain a lot of information about golf tees but very little about tea parties.'

'Oh,' the little creature said. 'Where would the tea-party book be, then?'

'Now, this is quite the conundrum,' I continued. 'You may need a book about leaves—'

'But I don't want to find out about trees. I want to find out about tea,' the Dormouse said.

'And how would you make tea without leaves?' I questioned.

'Ah,' the Dormouse said. 'So in which section will I find the books about leaves?'

'I'm afraid the leaves book has no information about parties. The party books are, of course, in the section for Partlies.'

'Partlies?' the Dormouse scoffed. 'Surely, that's not a word!'

'Of course it is. And there is a whole book dedicated to it,' I explained slowly to the simple mouse. 'It's a rather large book, I'm afraid – far too big for your paws, as it covers parties but also partly covers other things.'

'What other things?'

'I'm not sure,' I replied, shrugging my shoulders. 'I'm only partly the way through it.'

'Do you have a smaller book about parties?' he asked, shaking his head. The whiskers above his nose trembled like guitar strings as he got increasingly agitated. 'This library makes no sense at all!'

'Don't despair, Dormouse,' I reassured him, though I was quite miffed about his comment on my library. I chose to forgive the creature, as all good librarians do. 'I have books about small parties. Small books about parties. Small books about small parties—'

'This sounds like a lot more than seven books,' the Dormouse interrupted.

I leaned in close to the furry creature. 'That's because there are stories within stories, and stories within those.'

The Dormouse threw up his tiny arms. 'Never mind, Mock Turtle. I shall find what I need myself.'

'A book, you must understand, can be a terrible thing,' I repeated, calling out after him.

He darted across the library, through section after section, scampering over the spines and hopping between my seven books as I hurried behind.

He settled on the book about leaves. A good book. A

leading book on the subject of leaves. But when a book does not have the information one is looking for, one can be sucked into the wrong story, and what lies beyond can be mind-goggling.

As all inexperienced knowledge-seekers do, the Dormouse opened the book and disappeared inside.

'Dormouse?' I called out as the book closed shut behind him.

As I suspected, he had fallen into the wrong book, lost in a web of words and sentences he didn't need, and it would be some time until we saw him again.

If ever.

That is why you must trust your librarian guide. A good library needs a good librarian and, without one, what awaits can be quite terrible.

'Dormouse?' I called again. 'Dormouse?' I scoured the pages, one by one, looking for a lost creature among the leaves.

The library doors swung open again, and the Pigeon swooped in, bustling her babies for the toddler singalong and story time. She was a friendly bird, and we got along well, though I always had to remind myself not to mention my friend Alice as the Pigeon did not share my sentiment for the girl. Silly Alice had made the mistake of saying she enjoyed eating an egg or two when she'd met the Pigeon. She may as well have said, 'I'd rather like to eat your babies, alongside a cheese-and-pigeon-feather sandwich.'

'I must apologize,' I said to the Pigeon. 'I'm running rather late for the babies' sing-song. The Dormouse has disappeared into a book.'

'That's OK,' she said. 'In fact, I came across a book that needed returning, so perhaps I can help by putting the book away for you.'

'I don't believe this book is one of mine,' I said, glancing momentarily at the book but continuing to turn pages, trying to locate the lost Dormouse. 'I can account for all the books in my library. Perhaps someone else is missing a book?'

I left the Pigeon to tend to her squawking babies and continued to search for the Dormouse.

The Pigeon and her babies didn't stay long. The thing about squabs is that they are often hungry, and in a library like mine, full of juicy bookworms, I will not stand for beaks pecking at book spines, hunting for food. The Pigeon knew this, having been fined in the past, and herded up her children quickly before they could sniff out the juiciest of the worms.

The close of the day crept up on me, as it often does,

and I did what every good librarian does at that time after leaving their readers deep within the pages of their chosen books (where I was sure the Dormouse was probably feeling quite at home): I selected a book for myself and headed down to the beach.

What had I missed? What hadn't I noticed? Who would want to commit such a crime? I replayed the day leading to the missing book again.

The Gryphon. The Frog-Footman. The Dormouse. The Pigeon.

The Gryphon. The Frog-Footman. The Dormouse—

Just then, the library doors swung open, and the Gryphon burst in. 'I have read the stories you gave me yesterday, and I greatly enjoyed them,' he announced. 'Now, I would like to borrow another.'

The tears began to roll down my cheeks, soaking my flippers as I wiped at my eyes.

'Oh, Gryphon,' I sobbed. 'There is a missing book.'

He waited for me to dry my eyes. I filled him in on all that had happened the previous day and the sudden appearance of the missing book.

'How could this happen?' he demanded.

I told him about how I had counted the books, one

through to seven, and how I had then seen a book on the Missing Book shelf. And how seven books were no longer seven but instead seven and one.

'Have you retraced your steps?' the Gryphon asked.

'Well, of course I have,' I snapped. 'It's only the first thing one must do in their search for a lost item.'

I spoke of the visits from the Frog-Footman, the Dormouse and the Pigeon, and how they'd only led me right back to the Missing Books shelf and my unsolved conundrum.

'What kind of librarian allows a book to go missing?' I wailed.

I bawled a while longer as the Gryphon was unusually tender and rubbed my shell, like a mother soothes her child. He then tapped my head and cleared his throat.

'This shelf?' he asked gently, waving a wing at the ledge. 'This shelf right here?'

My gaze followed the direction of the Gryphon's large wing.

It was empty.

EMPTY!

The shelf was clear, hollow and dark. I jumped up and stuck my head right through the gap. In fact, the entire shelf was missing, just as any good Missing Book shelf should be. No spines, no pages, not even a splinter. The missing book was no longer on the missing shelf, which meant only one thing: it had been found. The book had an owner, a reader, someone to peruse its pages. This, as all librarians would agree, is truly a joyful moment.

'The book has been found!' I cried with glee.

The Gryphon grabbed my flippers, and we danced in circles as the tears that rolled upon my cheeks danced their own happy dance.

'What was the name of the missing book?' the Gryphon asked, as we slowed to a waltz.

I sat a moment and thought. 'I think it was a book stamped *Return to Wonderland*,' I replied slowly. I suddenly remembered the Pigeon saying she had found a book that needed to be returned.

I turned to the Gryphon and smiled. 'I believe now it has found its reader.'

Roll of Honour

by Patrice Lawrence

I first read Alice's Adventures in Wonderland *more than forty years ago and one of the most memorable scenes is the croquet game. What must it be like pottering around a grass field waiting to be thwacked by a flamingo? So, I thought, what if you were from a family of renowned croquet balls? How do you prepare if you know you have to face a very cross Duchess, an even crosser Queen and a positively furious flamingo? Suddenly, Honour Roll was born!*

Patrice Lawrence

Dear Diary,

You now belong to me. I've written my name – Honour – across your front, in case you forget. You are the last diary that Nana's ever going to get me. She says that time has a habit of running away from her, and all that chasing diaries up and down our street is making her joints hurt. Luckily you're quite a tame diary and happy for me to write in you. Please don't close your pages too quickly. I've got a fresh bottle of ink, and I'm using my best quill. I don't want everything to smudge.

I'm going to start by telling you about my family. We are the Rolls. I live with Mum, Dad, my nana and most of my brothers and sisters. My baby brothers are called Tuckan and Rockan. My older brother, Cheese, left the nest last month. He's on his nap year, trying out new hibernation spots across Wonderland. I share a bedroom with my older sister, Spring, if sharing a room means I get a patch about the size of Tuckan's nose, while Spring takes over the rest of it.

And there's me, of course. I'm Honour. Honour Roll.

We live along High Hedges with an array of other hedgehogs and curious animals. Mr Simeon, our neighbour on the right, is a skink. He does house repairs around Wonderland with his friend Bill. They're usually over at the Duchess's mansion because the cook's got a bit of a temper and keeps breaking things.

Mr Simeon's granddaughter, Taliqua, is in my class at school. The first time I met her, she stuck her tongue out at me. I almost drop-rolled on the spot. Her tongue's blue! She's not as weird as her friend Gertrude, though. She's a gecko and licks her own eyeballs.

High Hedges is a long street on the top of a hill with fields sloping down either side. Rockan and Tuckan's bedroom is at the back of the nest, and all the fields you can see out their window belong to the Queen of Hearts. Mine and Spring's room looks out over the Duchess's fields, right down to her pepper orchard at the bottom.

The Queen and the Duchess are always arguing. Nana says that they've been like that for as long as she can remember. Luckily they haven't had a battle since I've been born. I'm glad of that. High Hedges would be right in the middle of it.

But that's enough about my family and my home. There's something important happening this week. It's Wonderland's Spiky Animal Try-outs. Yes! The SATs. In

Teardrop Bay, the urchins are learning their quadrilles to see who will get to dance with the turtles. Down past the Queen's palace in Wellington Deep, the spiny mice are running tale-telling competitions to see who can tell the most boring story. Last year, the winner was so boring that the dormouse who was judging it fell asleep and never properly woke up.

We hedgehogs are trying out for the Queen of Hearts's croquet game. The Queen's croquet games are special. The mallets are elite fighter flamingos from the Queen's private flock. The hoops are soldiers, who keep shuffling about. And we – we are the balls. It's a long-standing tradition that a member of the Roll family is always selected for the top team. When Mum and Dad were hoglets, they were part of the High Hedges Sonic Six, famous for their speed and swerving skills. Last year, Spring won the Best Shot trophy, when the King of Hearts sent her flying through three hoops in a row. Even Cheese made it to the top team and managed to stop the Duchess from winning by spiking a hoop's ankle. The soldier had to go to first aid for a plaster.

The Queen has to win. All hedgehogs know that, and so do the flamingos. That means the flamingos should pretend to hit us and trust us to roll the right way.

Unfortunately, some flamingos really do like hitting us.

Dad's final game was famous. A really grumpy flamingo called Fred was the mallet. Fred really hated hedgehogs. Mum told us it was horrible to watch – Fred would arch his neck back as far as possible and swing down, beak first, like he was trying to chop Dad in half. Dad always managed to get away, except that last time. One of his prickles got caught on a clump of mud and wouldn't budge. He just had to curl up as tightly as he could.

Fred really wasn't expecting that. He was used to Dad rolling away at the last second. Fred slammed right into Dad and, well, Dad said he never knew that flamingos could make sounds like that. They had to take Fred away on a stretcher. Mum reckoned he looked like a giant pink salt shaker.

Fred retired, but he has a granddaughter called Inigo. She's playing in this year's competition. She hates hedgehogs as much as her granddad does.

Please don't tell anyone, Diary, but I don't know if I want to try out for the SATs. I'm a bit scared. I'm not fast or brave or clever like everyone else in my family. I don't want to face a frumious flamingo looking for revenge.

Dear Diary,

Thank you for opening at the right page. I'm really sorry I shut you in the drawer for the last couple of days. I've been trying to practise my croquet moves, but I'm still terrible.

The SATs are tomorrow.

After school today, I met up with my best friends, Dua and Duo Hartley. They're the Queen's butler's niece and nephew. They're also cards, so they know the deal. We found a spot near a deserted bandersnatch burrow halfway down the slope between High Hedges and the Duchess's pepper orchard. The fields near the pepper orchard can get a bit sneezy if the wind's blowing the wrong way. Today, there was just a little tingle, but not much else.

We started with the easy rolls. Duo and Dua took three steps away from each other, lifted their arms and leaned forward until they were palm to palm. I practised rolling towards them and going through. Except, I couldn't go through, no matter how wide apart they were. As soon as I got to the top of the hill, I couldn't control how fast I came down again and whizzed straight past the hoop. Every time.

As I trundled up the hill for the eleventh time, I heard a honk.

'Nice try, Spike Head.'

Inigo the flamingo swooped down and landed on the slope between me and the twins. She clapped her wings together slowly.

'I heard you Rolls were supposed to be the best! You've definitely gone downhill. That's going to make my granddad so happy.' Inigo swished her neck to and fro. 'You will be pleased to know that I've been making my own preparations for the game.'

Inigo lunged forward and headbutted the ground. It made a loud thud. As she straightened up, the sun glinted off her head. She was wearing a pink crash helmet.

Dua clapped her hand to her mouth. 'That's cheating!'

'How can it be cheating? I belong to the Queen, and the Queen makes the rules.' Inigo tapped the helmet with her wing tip. 'This is made from the strongest jabberwocky claw. It's completely hedgehog-proof and very, very hard.'

I felt myself bristle. 'I still think it's cheating.'

'Are you scared?' Inigo hopped closer to me and pushed her beaky face close to mine. 'Because you should be.'

Inigo soared up and away towards the Queen of Hearts's palace.

'Well,' Dua said. Her face was creased and red. 'That was just rude!'

I nodded, but I didn't feel like practising any more. Now I was even more scared than ever.

Dear Diary,

I'm sorry it's been three days. I haven't got bored and forgotten you like Nana said I would. Please believe me.

So much has happened since the last time I wrote. Well, first, I got through the SATs! I think I should feel happier about it than I do, but then I'm not so sure because *everyone* got through. Madame Pierce, my teacher, says they need more hedgehogs this year because there's going to be an epic battle between the Queen and the Duchess. That's because of the second thing that happened.

I was woken up the day after my rolling practice by a blast of trumpets. It sounded like they were coming from the pepper orchard. I peered out of my window. And then I sneezed so loud I woke up Spring. She rubbed her eyes and started sneezing too. It wasn't just us. I could hear Mum and Dad – and little baby sneezes from Tuckan and Rockan.

We rushed outside. I thought I was still asleep because the pepper orchard wasn't at the bottom of the hill any more. It was halfway up and moving closer to us. High

Hedges was filled with the sound of animals chattering and sneezing, trying to work out what was going on.

Mr Simeon emerged from his burrow. He slapped his hand to his forehead, making his eyes pop. 'So, it's really happening, then.'

The animals stopped chattering. (Though none of us could stop sneezing.)

'What do you mean?' Mum asked.

'You know I've been fixing things at the Duchess's house? Well, there I was, hammering in some brackets in the kitchen, when who should come on a visit? The Knave of Hearts. He acts the joker, but I've never trusted him. He hands the Duchess a scroll. The Duchess reads it, looks like she's going to explode and then tears it into tiny pieces. I catch the Knave as he's on his way out. This time, the Queen's said that if she wins she's going to take the Duchess's house and pepper orchards as a prize—'

Mr Simeon had to stop talking then because the sneezing was getting too loud.

'*If* she wins?' Mum said. 'The Queen *always* wins!'

'Exactly,' Dad said.

The pepper orchard had stopped moving. Suddenly, the hill was full of rabbits, all wearing tabards and carrying trumpets with banners decorated with the Duchess's emblem, a big red nose.

'Order!'

The rabbits arranged themselves into two rows, trumpets hanging by their sides. A tall black rabbit stepped forward.

'My name is Steve,' he said. 'I am the Duchess's Chief Trumpeter and Best Messenger.' He took a scroll from an inside pocket of his tabard. 'I come with an important message from the Duchess.'

He held the scroll so close to his face, his whiskers made the parchment twitch. We all waited and tried to hold back our sneezes. Steve cleared his throat.

'Her Right Honourable Lady Duchess of Sternutation does hereby lay claim to the allegiance of the curious creatures of High Hedge. It has come to the Right Honourable Lady Duchess's attention that the Queen of Hearts is a big scaredy-cat cheat who is afraid of losing. This year, the Duchess will win and calls upon every hedgehog in High Hedges to roll for her.'

He replaced the scroll in his secret pocket.

Mr Simeon scratched his head. 'You want us to help the Duchess stop the Queen winning?'

Steve nodded.

Mum shook her head. 'Well, Steve. Please tell the Duchess that we'd love to help, but we can't. The Queen has too much of a temper. We can't risk –' she looked to see if Tuckan and Rockan could hear – 'our necks.'

There was a murmur of sneezy agreement. Steve turned to face the rabbits behind him. He waved his paw, and they raced around to the back of the orchard. Steve blasted a note on his trumpet, and the rabbits started playing their instruments.

The pepper trees shivered again and ambled towards us. A big sneeze started at the back of my nose and burst out. It wasn't just me. Mr Simeon sneezed so hard I thought his eyes really were going to pop right out. Dad ushered the twins back into the nest.

Steve lifted his arms, and the trumpeters stopped. So did the pepper trees.

'We have been instructed to keep the pepper trees here,' Steve said. 'Until we have word from the Duchess that they can return.'

The sneezing was getting so bad that none of us could stay out any more. Spring and I looked out of our bedroom window at the dark shape of the trees.

'Don't worry about the Duchess,' Spring said. 'The Queen always gets her way. Just do what our family has always done. Roll for Queen and country. The Queen will make sure we're all right.'

Dear Diary,

I didn't know that diaries could sneeze too. The pages are a bit damp now, which is making my writing smudgy, but I'll carry on.

Today's the day of the croquet game. I wish it wasn't. Mum's made breakfast. It's snail porridge, my favourite, but I'm not hungry. I poked my nose outside the door earlier, but had to bring it inside again because of the pepper. Mr Simeon was already up with his tapeworm measure, trying to work out if the trees had moved any closer overnight. The tapeworm kept sneezing and making Mr Simeon even crosser.

OK. It's time to go. Wish me luck, Diary!

LATER

Even as I'm writing this all down, it feels like a dream. But I was there, and it really happened.

As we were heading to the Queen's palace, I still had no idea what I was going to do. Should I roll for the Duchess or for the Queen? The hedgehogs from the tulgey wood were wearing caps covered in hearts. So were the hedgehogs from the royal forest, of course. The Queen was going to win no matter what I did. I would do what the Rolls have always done. I'd make sure the Queen would win.

I hadn't been to the Queen's gardens before. Spring did warn me that it was a bit strange. There were fish in wigs and tailcoats and, even weirder, the Queen's roses leaked. I saw it with my own eyes: little puddles of red around the bottom of the trees. I arrived just as the Royal Family's procession was marching through the main entrance. I was keeping an eye out for Inigo, but the game stewards, all club cards, sent the flamingos to one end of the field and us hedgehogs to the other.

'Honour!' It was two voices, Duo and Dua.

'Guess what?' Duo said. 'The Queen's locked the Duchess in her pepper cellar! You know what that means, don't you?'

'The game's off?'

'No,' Dua said. 'The Queen's going to play against herself!'

'And the Duchess is more frumious than a bandersnatch with toothache,' Duo added.

'We've still got the pepper orchard on our doorstep,' I

said. 'And it's going to be there forever unless the Duchess orders it to go.'

We couldn't stay in High Hedges. We'd have to move away from our cosy nest and all my friends. But what could I do?

The game began. The club steward sent me to a hedge on the far side of the garden. I crouched down next to an abandoned spade sticking out of a hole. All the action was at the other end of the pitch, where the Queen had a crowd around her cheering her every move. It was a lot of cheering because she was doing all the moves.

'So! You think you can hide, do you?'

A long shadow fell over me. I looked up. Inigo was perched on the spade.

'I'm not hiding,' I said. 'I'm waiting to be played.'

'Well, I'm ready to play.'

Inigo swished her head. Her pink helmet shone. Suddenly, she swung at me. I managed to swerve to my right and her beak plunged into the grass. She freed herself quickly.

'My name is Inigo Flamingo. Your dad quilled my grandfather. Prepare to fly.'

Inigo came at me again. I tucked and spun forward, landing just by her chest. She looped her neck round between her spindly legs. Her upside-down face grinned at me. She straightened up and flew off the handle, diving towards me. I moved quickly, but the wrong way. I plopped down into the hole. I was stuck – I mean really stuck. My prickles were wedged in the mud, just like Dad's. I couldn't move.

Inigo drew herself up to her full height and tipped back her head. Her grin was so wide, it made her beak look like it had been turned sideways.

I closed my eyes.

'My name is Inigo Flamingo. Your dad quilled my grandfather. Prepare to – honk!'

'Got you!'

That wasn't Inigo's voice. I opened my eyes again. Inigo wasn't standing there any more. She was under the arm of – well – I don't know whose arm it was. It belonged to a girl in a blue dress and a white apron. Inigo's beak fell open in surprise.

The girl raised Inigo into the air. 'You're a very curious mallet,' she said. 'And that's a very curious ball, but everything is so different here.'

Inigo started wriggling, but it was too late. The girl lifted Inigo high, and I just had time to curl into the tightest ball before Inigo swung towards me. Then, *thwack*! I really was flying!

This is what I saw as I went spinning over the pitch.

The girl in the blue dress, eyes wide, as I spun away.

Two club stewards shuffling towards Inigo with a stretcher.

A giant grinning cat's head hovering in the middle of the field.

The King of Hearts nudging the Queen and pointing at me.

The Queen's back as she bent over to take a shot.

The Queen's back getting closer and closer and closer – until . . .

I hit her.

The Queen screamed, and suddenly we were flying together, my prickles stuck into the back of her dress. Her nose skimmed just above the ground as everyone on the pitch made way for us. Everyone, that is, apart from the Duchess, who was rushing up the hill towards us with the executioner by her side. (I later learned that she'd been freed to answer questions about the grinning cat's head.) But that didn't matter now. What mattered was that she didn't get out of our way.

The Duchess's mouth dropped open in shock. For a second, I thought she was going to swallow me whole, but with a loud '*Ooof!*' the Queen thumped into her. Then the three of us were flying together, the Duchess whooshing backwards down the hill.

I heard a shrill toot on a trumpet and then a clattering and shouting. Steve, the messenger rabbit, was waving his arms at us. When he saw we weren't stopping, he turned round and raced back to the Duchess's gardens followed by his musicians.

And the pepper trees were following, skidding back towards their home. My eyes, my nose and even my ears were stinging with pepper as we flew down the hill after them. We were flying lower and lower until we finally landed, sliding down the grass. Well, not *we*. The Duchess was sliding backwards on her bottom, and the Queen was sliding on her stomach. I was still stuck to the Queen's back.

We landed in a tangled heap against the orchard fence. The Queen gave an enormous sneeze, and I shot into the air and bounced along the grass and carried on rolling until, with a little *plop*, I dropped into the hollow by a bandersnatch burrow.

'Who did this to me?' the Queen shrieked. 'How dare they interrupt my game! Off with their head!'

I decided that my head and I would stay where they were for a while.

'If your game isn't finished,' the Duchess said, 'that means no one's won.'

There was silence. I risked peeking over the top of the burrow. The Queen was frowning.

'I think you're right,' she said grumpily. 'But, next year, beware. I will win!'

She shook a mist of pepper out of her skirts and stomped sneezily back up the hill.

'I think it's time to go home,' said a soft meowy voice.

The cat's head was hovering by the side of the Duchess. Slowly, more of its body appeared. Its paw patted the Duchess's back, and together they went through the gate to the orchard and closed it behind them.

It may be my imagination, but I'm sure the cat's head turned towards me and winked.

Dear Diary,

I was exhausted after yesterday, and I fell asleep with my quill in my paw. Thank you for staying open on the write page.

I'm going to put you back in the drawer for a little bit, as all the curious animals in High Hedges are throwing a tea party for me, and that's definitely not to be sneezed at.

The Tweedle Twins and the Case of the Colossal Crow

by Chris Smith

The Tweedles have been among us a rather long time – in fact, they were already over one hundred years old before Lewis Carroll corralled them into Wonderland.

They first appeared sometime in the 1700s (and I often feel the same myself on a Tuesday morning). Tweedle Dum and Tweedle Dee – back then – represented the bickering supporters of two rival musicians. Eighteenth-century fandoms, if you like. Fighting each other not with social media but with kitchen utensils, which strikes me as a good deal more civilized.

Alice seemed to warm to these two hotheads immediately, and so did I. Because – let's face it – there is a pair of Tweedles living inside each and every one of us. And dashed uncomfortable that can be too. I hope you enjoy their adventure as you go in search of your own personal crows and ride them unswervingly into the Pool of Ensmallment.

Chris Smith

In the middle of a field, in the rain, underneath two hats and a large black umbrella, and inside two shirts and two pairs of trousers (four trousers in total) stood two little men. They were as cold and soggy as a pair of abandoned trifles.

'I thought you said we would have an outstanding day today,' complained Tweedledee, shaking his right boot, which had filled with water.

'And so we are,' countered Tweedledum. 'We are out, standing in this field. And we are outstanding at it.'

'Contrariwise, we are terrible at it.' Tweedledee sneezed with a sound like wet cabbages being vigorously shaken.

'We must stand in the middle of the field,' his twin explained patiently, 'because it is our job. You told me yourself only this morning. We are scarecrows.'

Tweedledee sighed like an angry steam engine, rolling his eyes together. 'Scared of crows!' he retorted, his voice going up a full two octaves and scaring a robin that had been hanging around nearby. 'We are scared . . . of crows. Not scarecrows. Is that why we've spent the last four hours out here in the rain?'

Tweedledum looked slightly embarrassed, fiddling with his collar, upon which the word 'Dum' was embroidered in red thread. He coughed in the way that means, 'Errrrm . . . yes,' but is slightly less awkward to say.

'I don't want to!' screeched Tweedledee abruptly and at an even higher pitch, snatching the umbrella and squelching away through the mud. 'I don't want to be out standing in this field any more! I don't want to be a scarecrow!'

'Well, I don't want to be scared of crows,' said Tweedledum, hurrying after him. 'Nohow.'

'I demand a battle!'

'I'm too wet to battle!'

'I demand satisfaction!' Tweedledee's voice was now so-high pitched that it sounded like a kettle coming to the boil. His face was red and shining with fury – he looked like the angriest, ripest, most smartly dressed tomato you ever saw.

'We could battle the crow,' Tweedledum suggested suddenly.

By now, they had reached the fringes of the wood at the edge of the field, and they both stopped to shelter under the overhanging branches.

'Battle . . . the cr—argh?' his brother asked, so terrified to even utter the word out loud that he choked on the last syllable as if a small duck of fear had flown into his mouth.

The pair were terrorized on an almost-daily basis by a huge black crow, which came flapping and squawking at them like a bad memory – only one with wings and claws.

Involuntarily they both looked fearfully at the sky, then Tweedledum steeled himself.

'Yes, battle the crow,' he said decisively. 'For too long, we have been afraid of it. I say, let's go and find its nest and give it a good old scare. It's just a bully. And you know what they say about bullies?'

'You should run in zigzags to escape them because they can't turn corners very well?'

'No – that's crocodiles.'

'You should punch them in their sensitive noses?

'Mmm, you're thinking of sharks there.'

'You should wait until they're a nice yellow colour, then peel and eat them?'

'Bananas.'

'Ah. Well, in that case, no, I don't know what they say about bullies.'

'You should stand up to them!' declared Tweedledum, striking a dramatic pose, which made rainwater run off his cap and down the back of his neck. 'Let us gird up our loins, and all the other bits of us as well, and prepare for the Battle with the Colossal Crow!'

'Let us arm ourselves!' agreed Tweedledee, thinking that, if nothing else, it would warm him up a bit. 'Bolsters! String! Tanks!'

'We don't have tanks,' his brother told him sadly. 'But the rest we can do! To arms!'

'And legs!'

It took the Tweedle Twins some considerable time to prepare themselves for their dangerous quest. But eventually they were ready – both with thick blankets tied round their middles with string, and saucepans set firmly atop their heads.

'Onward,' ordered Tweedledum, 'and upward.'

'How do we know the crow is up there?' asked Tweedledee, peering through the tree trunks that marched away up the hill like thin green-haired soldiers with squirrels on.

'Anything worth questing for is always uphill,' explained the other. 'Nobody ever won a famous victory going downhill.'

'It feels like cheating, somehow,' agreed Tweedledee, and they started up the slope together, each jostling for second place in case the crow should suddenly appear.

'Don't be afraid,' urged Tweedledum, pushing his twin in front of him. 'You know what they say – a faint heart butters no parsnips. He who dares . . . is worth two in the bush.'

'I would *like* to be worth two in the bush,' said

Tweedledee uncertainly. 'And butter the parsnips too. But it's not easy being brave. Not when the crow is so very, very big. And I heard that many strange animals live in these woods.'

There was a sudden clap of thunder. Somewhere a cow barked. He was right about the strange animals.

'The woods are full of enemies, but never fear – I shall recite a poem to lift your spirits,' his brother reassured him. And, clasping his hands behind his back, he began:

> *Elephant, Elephant,*
> *Wilt thou be mine?*
> *Thou shalt not fling fishes,*
> *Nor yet count the kine.*
> *But sit in a bathtub,*
> *With bells in your hair,*
> *And feast upon clams,*
> *Like a millionaire.*

'That is not how the poem goes,' complained Tweedledee.

'Possibly not, but it is how it comes. To me at least,' explained Tweedledum.

By now, they were nearing the top of the hill, and the trees had begun to thin out as they approached a large clearing. The silvery glisten of water was visible through the undergrowth. Without warning, there was an apocalyptically loud '*KARK!*' from somewhere ahead.

(If you think about it, it's not that surprising that it was without warning. Crows don't gently clear their throats before they kark – not even giant ones. Or politely say in a soft voice, 'I'm about to utter an apocalyptically loud *kark*. I'm just letting you know in case anyone might be startled.')

The '*KARK*' was indeed without warning, and it operated on the Tweedles like an electric shock. They both leaped into the air with their hair standing on end. It was lucky that they were both wearing saucepans on their heads because they were standing underneath a low-hanging branch at the time.

Clang! went the saucepans as they hit the branch.

'*KARK!*' went the distant crow once again.

Clang! went the saucepans a second time.

This process was repeated for several minutes.

'How long are you going to be jumping into the air and hitting your heads on that branch?' asked a voice eventually from behind the Tweedles.

They both spun round and jumped again in surprise.

Standing behind them was a monkey, immaculately

dressed in a spotless white sailor's outfit.

'Why are you dressed as a sailor?' asked Tweedledum, deciding to start with the most obvious question.

The monkey blinked. 'Well,' it answered, 'you know what all the nice girls love, don't you?'

'A sailor?'

'No,' corrected the monkey, setting its hat at a slightly jauntier angle, 'a monkey dressed as a sailor.'

The brothers considered this statement and collectively decided that there was too much wrong with it to even begin a fruitful line of questioning. Instead Tweedledee asked, 'Do you know if this is where we can find the monstrously large crow?'

The monkey sucked in its breath theatrically, widening its little monkey eyes and dancing a brief, dramatic hornpipe. 'Oooooh,' it said, 'you seek the colossal crow?'

'Yes,' answered Tweedledee. 'I just said that.'

'Behold,' said the monkey even more dramatically, pulling a small brass telescope out of the pocket of its sailor suit and putting it up to its eye, 'the springs of different sizings!'

'Least catchy name ever,' complained Tweedledum, peering through the trees in the direction the monkey was looking.

As they inched forward, they could see that they had come to the edge of a large clearing. On the opposite side, set into a tall mossy bank, were two stone basins from which water was trickling. The streams filled two large pools in the centre of the clearing.

'Behold the Pool of Ensmallment!' breathed the monkey, using capital letters for extra emphasis.

It was pointing to the left-hand pond, which appeared to be empty. It was surrounded with what seemed at first sight to be tiny plants, like cress. But as the Tweedles looked more closely they could see that they were, in fact, perfect miniature trees clustered around the edges of the water, each no taller than one of your smallest fingers.

'And behold again, but this time, behold the Pool of Enlargement!' continued the monkey, gesturing with its telescope.

The right-hand pond was hard to make out because it was completely occupied by an enormous fish. The middle section of the fish was in the water, but its head and tail flopped out across the grassy clearing like a tall person trying to sleep in a baby's cot. The fish caught sight of them as they peeked through the trees and waved a large fin in greeting.

'Welcome!' the fish told them in a deep, rather pompous voice.

'Who are you?' questioned Tweedledee, forgetting about the crow in his curiosity and stepping forward out of the forest.

'I,' replied the fish grandly, 'am a big fish in a little pond.'

'Right,' said Tweedledee. 'That's more of a description than a name in the traditional sense, but anyway. Pleased to meet you.'

'Kindest regards,' added Tweedledum, moving out to join his twin.

'Have you come to seek enlargenment?' asked the fish seriously. 'Or to ensmallify yourselves?' Seeing their blank expressions, it went on, 'Drink from that pool over there, and you shall shrink. This one, however, will make you bigger. I myself jumped over from the other pool only this morning, and already I am several times larger and cleverer.'

'Cleverer?' Tweedledum frowned.

'You perhaps do not understand because of your size,' said the fish disapprovingly. 'But as I have grown larger my brain has swelled too, to an extremely clever size. Why, only just now, I thought of an excellent song within seconds, which I expect you would like to hear.'

Tweedledee was about to politely refuse, but the problem with big fish in small ponds is that they rarely listen to other people. The fish waved its fin again, calling for silence, and began to sing in an odd, high-pitched warbling voice:

> *Come, little prawns, and rest your heads,*
> *Warm and safe on the comfortable bread.*
> *Come, little prawns, and lie lengthways,*
> *'Neath a blanket of lovely soft mayonnaise,*
> *Sleep, little prawns, till morning.*
> *Sleep, little prawns, till dawning.*
> *Lay off your hard coats and your tickly legs,*
> *And curl up safe in the buttery bed.*
> *I shall pull a bread counterpane up to your chest,*
> *With a sprinkle of lemon to sweeten your rest.*
> *Sleep, little prawns, till dawning.*
> *Sleep, little prawns, till morning.*

'You are simply enticing those poor prawns into a sandwich!' burst out Tweedledee when the fish had finished. 'Why, that practically makes you a cannibal!'

'If you are going to be a cannibal, you may as well be practical about it,' reasoned the fish smugly, smacking its lips grotesquely. But the self-satisfied expression disappeared from its face as a terrifying sound came from close by, somewhere away to the right.

'KARK!'

'The crow!' panicked the fish, thrashing around in the pond like an overweight man in a paddling pool full of wasps. 'Flee! Flee for your very lives!' It eventually managed to flop its way out of the right-hand pool and began to roll itself across the clearing.

'Where are you going?' asked Tweedledee, hopping from foot to foot in panic.

'The crow drinks from the enlargening pool,' explained the fish as it rolled. 'Flee!' It flopped into the left-hand pond and began gulping at the water, growing noticeably smaller with each mouthful. Within seconds, it was the size of an averagely large fish – the sort that a fisherman might boast about catching. Then it was a size he would lie about. Then it was a size he would barely even mention. Then it was as big as a tadpole. Then it had vanished altogether.

'It's disappeared!' exclaimed Tweedledum.

'It's disappeared from sight,' corrected the monkey, which had climbed into a nearby tree and was hiding behind a large apple. 'That's quite different, you know.'

For a moment, Tweedledum pondered what had happened to the fish. *It has shrunk so much that it's no longer even a part of our world*, he thought to himself. *I wonder what it can see now?* The fish was, indeed, now a very small fish in what was, relatively, an infinitely large pond. But there was no time to think about it any further. With a thunder of wings that shook the branches around them, the gigantic crow landed in the centre of the clearing like a nightmare that someone had managed to glue feathers on to.

'*KARK!*' it explained.

These are the times when you really discover what sort of person you are. When you are being menaced by a giant crow and all help has vanished; the pompous fish has shrunk to microscopic size, and the sailor-uniform-clad monkey is concealing itself behind fruit. These are the moments when you have to show what you're made of. Tweedledum had spent his whole life being terrified of this black shadow that appeared out of the sky. But, suddenly coming face to beak with it in a forest clearing, he was surprised to discover that he was not afraid. Not as much as he'd expected to be, anyway.

The crow dipped its enormous head and took a great, slurping mouthful from the pool on the right of the clearing. It opened its wings and flapped them – and as the Tweedles watched, it visibly grew slightly larger.

'It drinks from the Pool of Enlargenment!' gasped Tweedledee, who had never been the fastest on the uptake. The rest of us had worked that out at least two pages ago.

'And that's why it's so big!' added Tweedledum, who was, if anything, slightly slower on the uptake than his brother, running on average about a paragraph behind.

'*KARK!*' agreed the crow, advancing towards them with its beak open. The beak – just to give you some context – was about the size of a dustbin. Easily big enough to swallow a boy whole, even a rather big one. And still leave room for a second boy as pudding, possibly with a scoop of ice cream on the side.

Tweedledum raced over to the trees at the edge of the clearing and began to climb as fast as he could.

'Oh great,' scoffed his brother, 'you're running away as well, are you? Thanks a lot. Well, if you think you're going to be able to hide behind an apple, you are much mistaken.'

But that was not Tweedledum's plan. As the crow passed underneath, stalking towards his brother like an embarrassing memory, he used a springy branch to *sproing* himself high into the air. Yes, it is a real word.

Tweedledum sailed through the air like a rugby ball with a hat on, landing perfectly on the back of the monstrous crow. The crow screeched in fury, thrashing its wings to try to dislodge its unwanted passenger. But Tweedledum held on tightly to a handful of feathers – and with his free hand, he reached into his pocket to grab his cloth cap, which he snagged neatly over the crow's eyes.

There followed what can only be described accurately as a crowdeo. In other words – a rodeo, only with a crow instead of a horse. The crow bucked and capered around the clearing, flailing its wings but not daring to take off without being able to see where it was going. Tweedledum held on quite literally for dear life, puffing out his cheeks in concentration, although I'm fairly sure that at one point he did let out an involuntary 'yee-hah!'. Well, you would, wouldn't you?

Tweedledee now joined in. Skipping and squealing, 'Over here, Mr Crow – come and eat me! Over here!' he lured the crow across the clearing, towards the left-hand pond.

And the plan worked perfectly. The furious crow followed the sound of his voice, but before it could reach him, it fell – *splash!* – into the Pool of Ensmallment, still with Tweedledum planted firmly on its back.

'*KARBBBRBBBBRRRBBBBBL*,' said the crow, which is what happens when you start to say 'kark' but fall into a pool of water halfway through. Tweedledum desperately held its beak under the surface until he felt the enormous bird gradually begin to shrink.

'It's working – it's working!' he cried out to his brother, who was hopping about on the bank in glee.

Before long, the crow was merely the size of a cow. Then it was the size of a large dog. Then a smaller dog. Then an even smaller dog. And then finally, it was the size of a crow. At this point, Tweedledum was able to pick it out of the water and set it on the edge of the pond, pulling his cap off its head.

'*Kark!*' said the normal-sized crow in a normal-sized voice.

'Now it's time for us to scare *you* for a change!' declared Tweedledee, pulling a wooden rattle out of his jacket pocket. With a glint of victory in his eyes, he spun the rattle, and the loud noise so terrified the normal-sized crow that it fled into the treetops, squawking in fright. Tweedledee dropped the rattle on to the forest floor and danced a capering jig of victory.

'You know, in life, we all have our giant crows to face,' said Tweedledum, squeezing water out of his cap. 'But when you meet them head-on you often realize that they aren't nearly as big as they first seemed. Or as scary.'

'Are you looking for morals again?' asked Tweedledee suspiciously. He finished his capering with a final flourish, which was accompanied by a splintering, cracking noise. It sounded almost exactly like the sound a wooden rattle makes when a large boy treads on it and breaks it.

'Did you just step on my rattle?' asked Tweedledum in an unnaturally quiet voice, his face turning pale with fury.

'Ummmm,' hedged his brother, trying unsuccessfully to push the broken pieces of the rattle into the pond with his foot.

'That was brand new!'

'Errrrrr . . .'

'Come here! I demand a battle! Where are you going? Come back! How dare you run away! Stand and fight!'

And the two Tweedles disappeared down the hill, running as fast as their stubby legs would carry them. The monkey, peeping out from behind its apple, watched them go. *One of them looks smaller than the other*, it thought to itself, adjusting its sailor hat.

During Tweedledum's drenching in the Pool of Ensmallment, it is possible that some of the water got into his mouth. So it could be that the monkey was right.

Perhaps, forever afterwards, the brothers were no longer exactly the same. Tweedledum was, perhaps, very slightly shorter than Tweedledee. I couldn't be sure – it's impossible to get them to stand still long enough to measure them.

But one thing at least was certain: it had definitely been the weirdest day of the week so far.

And it was still only Tuesday.

Ina Out of Wonderland

by Robin Stevens

Alice's Adventures in Wonderland *has always been more than just a book to me. I grew up in Pembroke College, Oxford, across the road from where the real Alice and her sisters had lived more than one hundred years before. My father was the Master of Pembroke and hers was the Dean of Christ Church – so I know all about being a little girl in the very mannered, very academic adult world of Oxford University. Because I spent a lot of time in Christ Church College and on Christ Church Meadow, Wonderland has always felt like a very real place to me. I've seen the tree where the Cheshire Cat vanishes. I imagined the Mock Turtle dancing on the banks of the Cherwell, and the Duchess playing croquet in the Christ Church quads.*

I knew I wanted to write a story that made Christ Church a part of Wonderland, and that featured the real Alice and her family. I discovered that Lewis Carroll met the eldest Liddell girl, Lorina, first, and (presumably) began to tell her stories before he knew Alice, and I began to wonder how she felt about her sister stealing the limelight in the final book. Then I saw Lewis Carroll's photograph of the three sisters, taken around the time that Alice's Adventures in Wonderland *was written. In it, Alice and Edith droop sulkily on a sofa while Lorina sits between them, her back furiously straight, staring down the camera like she's issuing a challenge. I knew that this was a girl who could not be pushed around – and I knew what story I wanted to tell.*

Robin Stevens

I was beginning to get very tired of reading, for my book had very small lettering and no pictures at all, when my little sister Alice snuffled in her sleep and gave a great fidgety turn of her head on my lap.

I looked up through the dappling sun on the river bank and saw a rabbit in a smart new waistcoat and a bright checked jacket. He was running away from us through the daisies, and, as I watched, he paused, staring down at the pocket watch in his hand.

'Oh dear! Oh dear! I shall be too late!' he cried.

Then he took one more bounding leap and vanished into his rabbit hole.

He had bought a new jacket since the last time I saw him.

Alice cried out, 'Ina!' at me and jumped like a fish, her hands making stars on the grass, and I knew that although she had not physically moved (as far as I could see), in her mind, she was falling down and down into Wonderland, a place that is at once further away than London and Paris and also no distance at all.

Wonderland is a place that I know an unfortunate amount about. It does not have rules or bounds. I have learned to my cost that it is everywhere and nowhere at once. It began as a story *He* told me, but it did not stay that way.

'Alice!' I said, and I shook her shoulder. 'Alice, wake up!'

But Alice did not wake. I had not really thought she would. She could not – not until Wonderland was done with her.

At that, my sorryness grew and spread until it filled me up inside. For I had not told Alice about Wonderland, not even once. I had practised before the mirror, many times, but I only sounded contrary, and I only looked sour. After all, how could I explain to Alice – or anyone – that a dreamland where you can have a tea party that never ends, play croquet with hedgehogs and dance to the Mock Turtle's song is a horrid, dangerous place, to be avoided at all costs?

And now Alice was lost in Wonderland too.

But instead of feeling hopeless, I found that I was filled with rage. I am the oldest. The one who can bear anything, and I do. For years, Wonderland has been catching up with me and toying with me like our cat, Dinah, toys with a mouse, and I am almost used to it . . . although I have fought the Jabberwock more times than I would have chosen, and I have been beheaded by the Red Queen more times than I care to admit.

I felt that it was most ill-mannered for Wonderland,

and *Him*, to now set upon my sister as well, for Alice is giddy and foolish and does not know a raven from a writing desk. Wonderland's madness would swallow her up like a whale does a fish.

At least, it would unless I did something about it.

And, at that moment, I resolved to. *He* should not always have everything his own way, after all.

So I leaned forward until my lips were almost at Alice's ear, and I whispered to her. I did not know if she could hear me, but I had to try.

'I *shall* help you, Alice,' I told her. 'Just remember to keep your head.'

And then I stood, gathered up my skirts and ran.

A student punting by 'hallo'ed at me cheerfully, splashing his pole about and nearly tipping himself into the water, but I ignored him. I scrambled up the bank and broke through the trees to see the golden stone walls of our Oxford College rising up like a ship, with the tall black hat of Tom Tower behind it. I shot past two fellows walking along the gravel path in their flapping gowns, heads bent, chattering like pigeons. I ducked right, past the timber and dust of the half-finished new buildings, through the little side gate, around the cathedral and up past the gardens into the echoing corridors that led to our deanery.

I dived past it, on up the stairs, round and round until
I was dizzy
And
Then
I
Arrived
At *His* front door.

I squeezed my fists together and tried to breathe calmly.
I remembered that in Wonderland I was the girl who had
outwitted the Hatter and beaten the Red Queen at chess.
I had done those things despite Him, so He ought to listen
to me now.

I rapped on the door, and it opened at once. He was
standing in the doorway just as though he knew to wait
for me, and behind Him was the nonsense of His room.
And on His desk I could see freshly inked pages: new
Wonderland stories.

I do think that He *looks* like a person from Wonderland.
He is fearfully thin with such a quantity of chestnut
hair, and He stands up ramrod straight. His hands were
splattered with ink, the nails all dark with it, and He was
frowning at me as though I had disturbed Him. I stared at
his fingers, and then at Him.

'You're writing stories again and putting Alice in them,' I said. I made it sound as though I was accusing Him, because I *was*.

'So I am,' he said. 'It's a pity you are no longer Liddell enough to enjoy Wonderland, Lorina, but luckily Alice is.'

I hate how he always twists words and names into something other than themselves. Words ought to *mean* something precise, but he makes them mean everything and so nothing at all.

'I'm exactly the right size!' I said. 'And even if I amn't, you've no right to put Alice into the story instead!'

'Alice is charmingly nonsensical, and she will fit nicely into Wonderland, better than *you* ever did. You will keep on misusing it and disobliging me, and you are far too grown up for children's stories, so here we are – and there she is. Here and there, and there and here, round and round in circles. If you think about it, Ina, you are really the one who has sent Alice to Wonderland.'

'That is absolute *nonsense*!' I cried. 'I didn't do anything! She's there because of you. Now let her out!'

'Once upon a time, you asked to be amused, and so I gave you Wonderland to amuse you, you contrary creature. Now you're unhappy because you have to share it with your sister? Do go away and let Alice be.'

He took me by the elbow and spun me back out into the corridor. The door slammed, and I was left staring up at it, feeling as though something had been taken away from me.

'I'll give you amusement!' I said to the closed door. 'I'll give you *grown up!*'

It was a very nice-sounding thing to say, but I did not know what on earth it could mean, and how else I could help Alice, until I was halfway down the stairs.

'Oh, my ears and whiskers!' I cried. 'Of course! I shall make her *too grown up to fit!*'

As I have said, there are no rules to Wonderland, and so there is no rule that says you mayn't trick it. I know perfectly well that Wonderland fits under and over and around our college, like two scrumpled bits of paper that have been pasted together rather lazily on a hot day, and so to move about at college is to move about in Wonderland.

I went barrelling all the way downstairs and through the front door of the deanery, interrupting an argument between our cat, Dinah, and Cook's friend's wire-haired puppy. The puppy yelped pitifully and nipped at my ankles, scampering out of the house towards the main quad. Dinah smirked at me and licked her lips, padding away to the garden.

I dashed on through the hallway and into the hot kitchen. Cook was in a rage about Dinah and the puppy, and she seemed to have spilt the pepper for the soup. It floated in the air, and I sneezed. And there, on the table, was what I wanted. Little slices of cake set out ready for Mother's tea.

I swooped on one of them and carried it away, with Cook's cries of, 'LORINA! PUT THAT BACK!' billowing after me. I snatched up the key to the airing cupboard from its place on the sideboard and took everything into the nursery, where I would not be disturbed.

In Wonderland, anything you like can be true, and anything can be false, just by saying so. So I took up my other sister Edith's paintbrush from the nursery table and painted 'Eat Me' on the cake. I held the cake in one hand and the key in the other and stared at them.

There is a trick to talking to things that I have learned in Wonderland. It is very similar to the way that grown-ups talk to very little children, and it is enormously useful. You simply do not even entertain the notion that you will not be listened to.

'You,' I told the cake sternly, 'are an expanding cake,

and you are delicious. You will find Alice, wherever she is, and you will make her eat you all up, and she will grow and grow and grow.'

I turned to the key. 'And you,' I told it just as firmly, 'are golden and delightful, and you will take Alice where she needs to go as quickly as possible.'

The key and the cake quivered, very gently, in my hands and then went still.

'Good!' I said, as though my heart was not pounding, for although I had sometimes twisted His stories, I had never played with Wonderland from the outside before. I walked back out into the dark little deanery hallway, oak-beamed and hung about with a row of dim lamps, and turned to face our three-legged hall table. 'Now, I shall put you down on this little glass table, and you shall find Alice at once.'

Even after everything, I hardly thought it would work. But, as I watched, the cake and the key suddenly pulsed, and the lamps above my head pulsed too, and then both little objects faded quite away on the table and were gone. It was as upside-down a vision as if one of Dinah's mice had suddenly turned about and bitten off her own tail.

'Good gracious!' I said to myself. The beginning of my nonsensical plan had worked. 'Whatever shall I do *now?*'

As I said it, I happened to look up into the looking-glass hanging over the hall table in its gilt frame. My looking-glass self stared back. I never like to see myself in pictures, but I like how I look in mirrors. I look like a girl who is not afraid of anything.

'Whatever shall I do now?' I asked myself again.

'There is only one thing to do,' said myself. 'You must be quite as wicked as you can be – wicked enough to be sent to bed for a week. That is the only way to get through to Alice.'

I realized that I was quite right.

I spun about on my heel and rushed out of the deanery as quick as winking, out into the huge main quad. It is as flat as a map, with a scroll of green grass trimmed by an army of gardeners, and an enormous fountain with a winged statue in its very middle.

I picked up my skirts and set my teeth, and I ran so fast that my feet in their boots twinkled across the grass. The gardeners bellowed, and the dons roared, for no one goes on the grass, most especially not little girls.

But faster and faster I ran, fast enough to feel as though I might fly, as though Wonderland was at my back and all around me – which I knew it *was* – and I leaped into the air and jumped with a great SPLASH into the fountain.

The sunlight around me vanished just as though someone had cut it out with scissors, and then I was falling into deep water that was salty on my lips. I heard the sounds of other creatures struggling to swim in the sea around me as I kicked and gulped and blinked droplets out of my eyes.

There was something wrong with my arms, I noticed with the odd calm that always comes over me when I fall into Wonderland. In fact, they were not arms at all, but bright green wings, and my nose was a nose no longer, but a curved red beak. I appeared to be a sort of exotic bird. It was another one of His jokes, of course.

A guinea pig swam by me, squeaking, 'Pardon!' And then an owl struggled past – and then I caught sight of Alice, tiny as anything, in pursuit of a plump little mouse.

'Alice!' I squawked. 'Alice, you are much too small! You must *grow* to get out! Listen to me!'

But Alice ignored me and struck out for the shore.

I followed her.

'Do go away!' said Alice, once we were both out on dry land.

I shook my feathers crossly. 'I shan't!' I said. 'Do listen, Alice. If you get big enough, Wonderland can't hold you any more. It's the only way out. But, until you *can* get big, remember to speak politely, and do not listen to nonsense, and *never* lose your head.'

'I'm sure I don't know what you mean,' said Alice pertly.

I snapped my beak at her. I was not sure if she saw who I was, or if Wonderland's trickery had confused her.

'Alice! I am older than you, and I must know better!' I cried – and at that moment, something closed round my arm like a vice, and I was dragged out of Wonderland back into the sun.

I was exceedingly wet, and my skirts and hair were all draggled around me. I was a girl again, I noticed, and I was quite pleased about that. But I was less pleased to find that *He* had hold of me.

'You meddlesome creature!' *He* hissed in my ear. 'Stay out of this story!'

'I certainly won't!' I snapped at Him, feeling exceedingly contrary. 'Anyway, what kind of *Ina* would I be if I stayed *out* of things?'

He snarled at me.

'I don't suppose you like me playing with words, do you?' I said triumphantly. 'Well, if that's so, you shouldn't have taught me to.'

There was a disturbance in the air above me, and a shadow loomed over my feet.

'LORINA LIDDELL!' bellowed my father, his bush of white hair trembling with rage. 'WHY?'

'I found the child in the fountain, Dean, and got her out,' said He.

'Very good of you, Dodgson,' said my father. 'Lorina, STAND UP.'

I stood, dripping.

'WHAT IS THE MEANING OF THIS?'

'No meaning,' I said. 'I tripped.'

'I can tell you are lying,' said my father. 'Lorina, you troublesome girl, why can't you be more like your sister?'

'If I were more like she, then she should have to be more like me, and no one wants that,' I said rudely.

'*LORINA!*' roared my father.

'She is at an awkward age,' said He.

'She always has been,' said my father. 'She is an awkward child. Go away, Lorina. I shall decide how to punish you later.'

My father turned to speak to Him, and while He was occupied I ran. Fountain weed had got uncomfortably into the neck and waist of my dress, but I ignored it.

I thought that I had done enough – but I could not quite be sure.

*

There was another thing I wanted to try to give Alice every possible chance.

Back to the deanery again I went, leaving wet footprints on the hall tiles, through the kitchen (pepper all around me) and out into the deanery garden.

As I knew she would be, Dinah was there, stalking a lizard who was sunning itself on the cucumber frames.

'Dinah!' I said. 'Wicked Dinah! Come here!'

Dinah hissed at me as the lizard fled.

'Nonsense,' I said to her sternly. 'Don't complain at me, madam. I need you.'

'Prrrowt,' said Dinah, flouncing her tail.

'Hush,' I told her, and I picked her up by her fat furry middle – she was about to have kittens again.

She sagged in my arms and gently bit my wrist.

'Now, Dinah,' I told her as I carried her across the garden. I was using my grown-up ordering voice again. 'Listen to me *extremely* carefully. It is absolutely essential that you go into Wonderland and help Alice there. Do you understand? Make her as big and as strong as you can, and *don't* let her lose her head.'

'Rrrrow,' said Dinah, baring her teeth in a smile.

I put her into the crook of the garden tree, her favourite perch, and tapped her sternly on the nose. 'Go on!' I said.

And, as I watched, Dinah faded from view. Her smile went first, and then her velvety paws. The tip of her tail was just vanishing as the deanery door was thrown open, and my mother came marching out into the garden. She had heard about the fountain.

'LORINA LIDDELL!' she screamed. 'COME HERE!'

'I shan't!' I cried, filled with boldness, and I ran as fast as I could – I had been doing rather a lot of running, and it was almost enough to dry me off – for the *other* door in the garden, the one that Alice and Edith and I have been expressly forbidden from ever going through.

It is always locked, and I knew that I would have to call on Wonderland one last time.

'Open up!' I shouted at it. 'Open for me at *once!*'

And the door opened. Before me stood the manicured hedges and the rows upon rows of red and white roses of the dean's private garden. It was not a place for little girls – *But I*, I thought, *am not a little girl any more. I am as big as anything.*

My mother shouted behind me. The gardeners shouted around me. I left footprints on the grass and scattered rose petals in the air. Some of them caught on my dress and in my hair.

Then I was out the other side of the garden, through

the door that leads to the meadow, pelting back along the sandy path towards the river bank. I had to hurry. I had to see whether what I had done had worked – if Alice was safely home again.

At last, I slid down the bank, panting and sweating and shedding leaves and petals on to the grass. There was Alice, still asleep just where I had left her, her arm thrown up to shield her face. I bent over her, my heart beating, and a few more red petals floated down on to her cheek.

Alice opened her eyes and blinked up at me.

'Wake up, Alice dear!' I said to her. 'Why, what a long sleep you've had!'

'I had the strangest dream!' Alice sighed, rubbing her hands over her face and disarranging her short dark hair. 'There was a rabbit, and a cat, and a garden, and I shrank, and then I grew and grew and *grew* – and now I'm here again!'

'Alice!' I cried happily. 'I believe you kept your head!'

'Of course I did,' said Alice, wrinkling up her nose. 'But what would you know? You're too big to have dreams like this one any more.'

Plum Cakes at Dawn

Or, What Happened When the Dormouse Went to Night Court

by Lauren St John

What I adore most about Alice's Adventures in Wonderland *is the sheer exuberance of Lewis Carroll's prose and characters and the delicious sense that absolutely anything is possible and indeed probable. As one fantastical event follows another and the Queen and various animals become increasingly hotheaded and irrational, I love it that for the most part Alice – and, in his brief appearances, the Dormouse – greets each fresh triumph or disaster with equanimity, polite curiosity and, quite often, a charming sweetness. Since the Dormouse is forever dozing, I thought that a bout of insomnia might allow him to experience some of the fun of which he's missed out. I hope very much that you enjoy it.*

Lauren St John

The Dormouse awoke with a sneeze and a splutter. His ribs twitched from being tickled, and his tummy hurt from being poked, and his tail ached from being pulled. The other animals peered down at him as if he were an exhibit in a science museum.

'What?' he cried. 'What have I missed?'

'Taxes are up; wages are down,' the Goat said gloomily.

The Dormouse didn't pay any taxes or earn a wage, but he squeaked with horror to show his support and dozed off again.

When next he opened his eyes, the animals were shaking their heads in sorrow.

'What? What have I missed?'

'The price of nuts has gone nuts,' the Squirrel said bitterly, 'and the chances of you and I ending up as a snack for a Hawk Monster have increased by five hundred and thirty-two per cent.'

This time, the Dormouse's squeak of horror was genuine. Unable to bear it, he went back to sleep at once.

He was woken a minute later by a fearful clanking and screeching. A knight in an ill-fitting suit of armour came trotting out of the forest on a Palomino stallion. He was brandishing a newspaper and yelling, 'EXTRA! EXTRA! READ ALL ABOUT IT!'

The Dodo burst from his burrow, stumpy wings covering his ears. 'Dear sir, might I suggest that you apply oil to your kneecaps and breastplate before you and your horse go stone deaf.'

'Pardon?' said the Knight.

'It's too late,' declared the Goat. 'He and his horse are already deafer than a yew tree and candyfloss combined.'

With the ghastliest crashing, grinding, neighing and stamping that ever tormented an eardrum, the Palomino pranced to a halt, whereupon the Knight unfurled a banner: TRIAL OF THE CENTURY! THE QUEEN VS THE QUEEN.

'WONDERLAND DAILY NEWS EXCLUSIVE,' yelled the Knight. 'THE QUEEN IS BATTLING THE QUEEN. WATCH THEM FIGHT TO THE DEATH. PISTOLS AND PLUM CAKES AT DAWN.'

The Dormouse wanted nothing more than to return to dreamland and erase this whole nightmarish episode from his head, but there was no chance of a lie-in while such a cacophony was terrifying the very birds from the trees.

'Why is the Queen fighting herself?' he asked his dear friend the Dodo.

A soldier who was snoozing, unshaven, beneath a bush,

sat up and said rudely, 'What a stupid question. This is why you animals are known as dumb beasts. *Of course* the Queen is not battling the Queen. The Queen Bee is suing *the* Queen. Isn't that obvious?'

'I'm not sure it is,' said the Dodo, adjusting his glasses. 'Why, if I may be so bold, is the Queen Bee suing *the* Queen?'

'How should I know?' snapped the soldier. 'All I've been told is that the trial starts at one minute to midnight at the Night Court. Be there or be a Dodo all your life. See if I care.'

An instant later, he was snoring under a silver birch.

The Dormouse fully sympathized with him and fervently wished that he could be snoring too. Sadly, the animals were in an uproar over the battling queens. Slumber was quite impossible.

The White Rabbit dashed past them in a panic, clutching a broken pocket watch. 'Oh, no, it's late. I'm in a state and so irate. Why, oh why, did I trip over the grate?'

Before anyone could offer advice, he was gone in a blur, his white tail bobbing in the direction of the town square. The Knight and his steed clanked and neighed after him. The Goat and the Squirrel followed, though rather more sedately.

As darkness descended, the Dormouse curled up in his nest and tried every conceivable cure for insomnia: pie crust, macadamia nuts, full-fat cheese and a documentary on slow-worms. Nothing helped.

The Dodo felt for him. 'Why don't you accompany me to the Night Court?' he suggested. 'Court cases are among the most tedious experiences in the universe. If warring queens don't send you to sleep, nothing will.'

The first difficulty was getting there. The Dormouse's legs were too tiny to walk the length of the royal estate. Unfortunately, the river taxi service had closed down because the fish had taken to riding bicycles.

In the end, they persuaded a wily trout in an oxygen mask to take them on a rickshaw for three times the usual fare. The Trout moaned the whole way. 'I don't know what the river is coming to. There are more balloons than bass. Comes to something when it's safer on the land than it is in the water.'

The Dormouse had hoped that the rocking of the rickshaw would soothe him to sleep, but it wasn't to be. He grew desperate.

'You're looking at life in a tail-about-nose kind of way,' the Dodo told him. 'Try topsy-turvy instead. You're forever nodding off and missing fantastical events. Aren't you fed up with it?'

The Dormouse was. He was also heartily sick of being tickled awake. He resolved to stay up for the rest of his days and enjoy every adventure Wonderland had to offer, starting with the Night Court. 'Bring it on!' he squeaked.

'Good mouse,' the Dodo said approvingly. 'There'll be time enough to sleep when you're dead.'

The Trout braked so suddenly that the Dormouse and Dodo were catapulted over the handlebars. A crowd was surging towards the courthouse across a garden lit by fireflies. The Knave of Hearts clutched a flaming torch, and the March Hare raced in circles. For safety, the Dormouse sat on the Dodo's head.

The courthouse was nothing like the Oak Tree Court to which the Dormouse was accustomed. It was a vast round room with many tiers of benches, one half crammed with the Mad Hatter and his friends, and the other with mock turtles and other creatures.

There was also an enormous tank in which twelve dolphins glided and turned triple somersaults.

'We've been conned,' the Dodo said with disappointment. 'The Trout has brought us to an aquarium.'

'Those show-offs are the jurors,' grumbled the Sheep, who was knitting furiously. 'The lawyers had a beast of a time finding dolphins that didn't know everything about everything. Luckily, a fisherman happened upon these in an unexplored lagoon in Pixienesia.'

She gestured at the floor, and the Dormouse saw that it was a giant map of Wonderland. Pixienesia was a rare paradise in the turquoise waters of the Spacific. Elsewhere in Wonderland, fires kept breaking out in the south and west, and the Mock Turtle had forecast tsunamis and flooding in the north and east.

'These dolphins had never heard of *the* Queen, much less the Queen Bee,' the Sheep went on. 'Their only fault is that they're eternally optimistic. But then nobody's perfect.'

'All rise for Judge Eagleburger,' barked a clerk, and the White Rabbit blew his trumpet.

The Dormouse shuddered at the word *eagle*, but an ancient man in a black robe tottered to the judge's bench. Once seated, only the top of his crooked grey wig was visible.

'Won't his size be a problem?' ventured the Dormouse.

The Dodo was extremely offended. 'What do you have against the vertically challenged?'

'Nothing, I—'

'ORDER IN THE COURT!' barked the clerk. 'In the case of *the* Queen –' he bowed deeply – 'versus the Queen Bee –' he waved dismissively at a beehive – '*the* Queen will be represented by Darius Shifty.' He beamed as a smarmy man in a pin-striped suit and red tie swaggered in.

'The *insects*,' the clerk sneered, 'will be represented by a bird – if it doesn't eat them first. Ha ha!'

A stray bee stung him on the behind to teach him some respect, and he ran wailing from the court. A new clerk seamlessly replaced him.

A raven walked with quiet confidence to the front of the court.

'That's Raven Black,' the Sheep confided to the Dormouse and the Dodo. 'The bees chose Mr Black because he can remember nine things at once. The Judge can only remember five: tea, milk, sugar, shortbread and retirement.'

'How many can Mr Shifty remember?' asked the Dodo, watching the lawyer sneak a sip from a hip flask.

'One – if he's lucky,' the Sheep said sourly.

The Dodo and Dormouse cast a worried glance at *the* Queen, who was seated on a gold chair, wearing a periwinkle-blue dress, pearls and a simple diamond-and-ruby crown. The King was sprawled at her side in his naval uniform, looking baffled.

Mr Raven Black began: 'On May twelfth, after the King had ordered the beheading of the last of the palace gardeners—'

'What of it?' the King said sulkily.

'. . . *the* Queen commanded a scullery maid to lop the head off every flower in the palace gardens,' continued Raven Black.

'Why am I being bothered with this trifle?' screamed the Queen.

'Your Majesty, we are here to determine whether or not you have the right to continue living in such a grand manner and ruling over the Queen Bee and her family when you're the sort of person who stops dahlias singing and, therefore, starves bees.'

'Who gives a fig about one or two flowers when there are a trillion others?' shrieked the Queen. 'And whoever heard of a dahlia singing?'

Raven Black put a potted plant on the witness stand. 'Ms Dahlia, what would you say to Her Majesty's question, "Whoever heard of a dahlia singing?"'

'I'd say she must be as deaf as a knight in a rusty suit of armour.'

The Knight rose to protest, but the weight of his helmet caused him collapse back into his seat with the noise of ten thousand falling saucepans.

'Order in the court!' pleaded the Judge, but nobody heard.

When at last there was only the whimpering of bats with burst eardrums, the Dahlia continued: 'Every flower can sing better than any choir of angels. Well, except for the Red Hot Pokers – they make a noise like a chainsaw. The rest of us sing for the joy of seeing the rising sun and to make our friends the bees happy. They need us to stay alive, and we need them.'

'Thanks, Ms Dahlia,' said Raven Black. 'My next witness is the Queen Bee. Do you solemnly swear to give the truth, the whole truth and nothing but the truth, my lady?'

'I do, Mr Black,' said a muffled but dignified voice from within the hive.

'Why are you suing *the* Queen?'

'Because, in common with many of her species, she lacks the wisdom or kindness to have power over us. Were that not the case, she would not have instructed her late Head Gardener to put weed killer on the lettuces, destroying seventeen hives of bees.'

'What of it?' the Queen replied haughtily.

'Because without bees there'll be no flowers, birds or honey,' the Queen Bee said tearfully. 'Everyone knows that honey is better than money.'

'It most certainly is not,' huffed the King. 'I'd rather eat fifty-pound notes spread with Marmite any day of the week.'

'I am rather partial to honey,' confessed the Queen, 'but I can easily switch to jam tarts, avocado on rye, plum cake or English muffins with smoked salmon and cream cheese.'

She started to drool, which was not dignified in the least.

'I'm afraid that won't be possible,' the Queen Bee. 'Without bees to pollinate fruit trees and crops, there'll be no strawberries, avocados or plums, nor wheat or rye to make tarts, muffins or cake, or feed the cows or goats that make cream cheese. If you can't grasp basic science, you are not fit to rule over my bees.'

The Queen was apoplectic. 'I know more about science than a MUCLEAR FIZZ-ASSIST. I can tell a rose from a daisy. Can you?'

There was a smile in the Queen Bee's voice. 'You mean, can I tell a *Rosa auscrim* from a *Bellis perennis*?'

'If you speak French again, I'll have you beheaded!'

screeched the Queen. 'What have the French ever done for us apart from eat snails?'

'Objection!' cried Darius Shifty. 'I'm absolutely mad about snails sautéed in garlic.'

The blackbirds agreed, although they preferred them raw.

'In fact, I was speaking Latin,' the Queen Bee told the Queen. 'The point, Your Honour, is that my most humble worker bee is vastly more intelligent than any royal. If the Queen knows so much about *physics*, she'll be aware that the hexagon in honeycomb is believed to be the most perfect shape in all of nature.'

'Thank you, my lady,' said Raven Black. 'Your Honour, I rest my case. Your Honour . . . are you asleep?'

'Don't be impertinent or I'll lock you up and throw away the key,' ranted Judge Eagleburger, smothering a yawn. 'Dolphins of the Jury, have you reached a verdict?'

'Yes, Your Honour. We find *the* Queen to be a dimwit unequal to the challenge of anything harder than catching sardines, and possibly not even that. By no means should she be living in splendour or ruling over anyone with more personality than a jellyfish.'

'Off with his flippers!' screamed the Queen. 'Battered dolphin and chips for tea.'

Judge Eagleburger bashed his gavel. 'Silence, Your Majesty, or I'll hold you in contempt. I sentence you to be stripped of your palaces and ermine robes. All gold and jewels must be sold in aid of a bee charity.'

'Yay!' cheered the Dormouse, wondering why no one else was celebrating as the Queen had hysterics and was taken away by soldiers. 'The bees won!'

The Sheep shushed him. 'The trial isn't over. This is just the first case of the night. This is not about warring queens and lame-brained kings. It's All Animals versus Almost All Humans. At stake is life itself.'

As the Dormouse prayed once more for sleep, a strong smell of burning arose from one side of the Wonderland map, and water began to gush out of the other.

Raven Black approached the bench. 'Your Honour, I implore you to halt the trial. There are wildfires in Chilli and Chimesia, and a monsoon has caused flooding in Myndia.'

'Never heard of them,' snuffled the Judge. 'The trial must go on. Next, we have Foxes & Friends versus the Hunters. Call your first witness, Mr Shifty.'

'We absolutely must hunt foxes!' roared the Master of Hounds. 'The dogs would be bored senseless otherwise. Besides, foxes eat chickens.'

A fox took the stand. 'You eat chickens too,' he said smoothly.

'That's different,' insisted the Master. 'Foxes, like mice, are vermin.'

The Dormouse squeaked with alarm at this and at the rising waters, which swept him and the Dodo past the Gryphon on a brisk current.

Raven Black said, 'Who decides?'

'What-oh?' roared the Master of Hounds.

'Who decides which animals are to be treasured and which are to be eaten or dragged from their dens?'

'What an extraordinary question! Everyone knows that Cheshire Cats, the Queen's horses, retrievers, beagles and labradoodles are to be cherished, while foxes, rodents, pigs, carthorses, pigeons, pheasant, ducks, deer, mongrels and March Hares should be shot, abandoned on the roadside, or fried for breakfast.'

The Fox said, 'But how do you decide who to kill or keep? Is it intelligence? Any fox or mouse is miles smarter, faster and more cunning than any spaniel. Is it looks? I see the Duchess is wearing the pelt of my cousin, Renard, as a scarf, so she must think our red fur handsome?'

'Madam, why do you wear fur?' Raven Black asked the Duchess.

'It's fashionable,' she snarled. 'Frankly, mink and tigers that don't want to give up their fur are selfish. Bald people manage perfectly well and save a fortune on shampoo.'

Raven Black turned to the Master of Hounds. 'Sir, why do you put antlers on your wall?'

'Any imbecile knows they're cheaper than chandeliers!' roared the Master. 'What use are they to deer anyhow?'

'We need them for fighting and—' began the Stag.

The Master butted in: 'Fighting is wrong.'

'*You* do it,' the Stag pointed out.

'That's different.'

By now, the smoke on one side of the courtroom was so thick that the Mad Hatter and Knave of Hearts were wearing masks. The Sheep was up to its belly in muddy water and struggling to keep its knitting dry.

Raven Black said, 'Your Honour, I beg you to stop the trial. There are floods in Llamarama . . .'

'Never heard of it.'

'. . . and every home has been razed to the ground in Caldermania.'

Judge Eagleburger paled. 'Will there still be unicorns?'

'Almost certainly,' lied Mr Shifty.

'Then the trial must go on. Next, the Polar Bears are suing the People.'

The Dormouse was certain he was hallucinating. He was now sitting on top of a paddling Dodo, alongside a duck, a flamingo and an anxiously floating walrus.

A polar bear took the stand and told heart-rending stories about losing her loved ones to hunger and loneliness as the ice melted and whales were hunted to extinction in Polarfornia. 'Please, people, consider the plight of my cubs – and yours,' she wept. 'Let's save Wonderland.'

'Yeah, yeah,' jeered Darius Shifty, summoning the King. 'How do you feel about the melting of the Polarfornia ice caps, Your Majesty?'

'Jolly glad you asked,' the King said importantly. 'Melting ice is infinitely better in a mulberry wine spritzer. It's easier to get in the glass. Anyway, how can you say Wonderland is overheating when just last week my favourite toboggan and three soldiers were buried in an avalanche?'

'I rest my case, Your Honour,' Mr Shifty said triumphantly.

'And I mine,' Raven Black said with sadness.

The water was now so high that the Judge was in a rowing boat, and the dolphins had left their tank and were leaping over heads. The Dormouse felt quite dizzy. Over the crashing of waves and wailing of fire engines, Judge Eagleburger shouted, 'Dolphins of the Jury, have you reached a verdict?'

"Your Honour, we find that anyone dull enough to drag innocent creatures from their burrows, hang antlers on their walls, or prefer crushed ice to happy bees, dahlias and polar bears should be banished to Pluto and never again given power over anything more exacting than fish guts. Nurses, librarians and unicorn-wranglers aside, humans are no good for anything apart from making plum cake and providing sanctuary for obese golden retrievers. Clearly, animals are superior in every way.'

Creatures of all shapes and sizes erupted in wild jubilation.

'Animals rule Wonderland!' the Walrus cheered.

The Judge bashed an oar on the prow of his boat. 'Mr Shifty has appealed on the grounds that Raven Black is cleverer than he is and, therefore, had an unfair advantage. I declare a mistrial. The Queen and Lesser Mortals will continue to rule Wonderland.'

Back in his nest, an immense weariness came over the Dormouse. His eyelids drooped, and he wished the White Rabbit would stop rushing about the forest reporting that the royals had had their heads chopped off by accident before the verdict was overturned.

Unluckily, Dinah, the cat, was being sworn in as Queen because no one else could be found of sufficient entitlement.

The Dormouse had drunk a lot of lavender tea. He was not entirely sure he was still conscious when the Dodo, in despair over the cruel verdict, decided that he would ask Alice, the girl who'd dreamed of being a scientist or, perhaps, a novelist, to bring *Tyrannosaurus rex* back from the dead to help the Planet sue the People.

'Are you mad?' said the White Rabbit, panicking. 'It'll crush us underfoot and devour us with one bite.'

'True, true.' The Dodo frowned. 'I'll specify that it must be hamster-sized.'

The Dormouse said sleepily, 'If Alice is to bring any animal back from extinction, wouldn't you prefer a dodo friend?'

The Dodo was insulted. 'I don't need the competition.'

At that point, sleep blessedly claimed the Dormouse. His eyes squeezed shut. 'Wake me up when it's all over,' he murmured, 'and only for good news.'

The Knave of Hearts

by Lisa Thompson

When I revisited Alice's Adventures in Wonderland, *it struck me that we never hear the final verdict in the trial of the Knave of Hearts. He stands accused of stealing the Queen's jam tarts, yet we are distracted from the case by Alice growing bigger and bigger and the cascading of the pack of cards. She awakes by the bank and we forget all about the Knave and his trial. Was he found innocent or guilty of the crime? Does he still have his head? This character was a gift. With the Knave of Hearts telling his own story I could use one of my favourite writing voices – the unreliable narrator . . .*

Lisa Thompson

I quite like my head. In fact, I'd say I'm rather attached to it. My chin is pointy, and when I walk into a room, my nose arrives well before my eyes do. But, all in all, I think it's rather a splendid head. It seems unbelievable to think that once upon a time our remarkable and extremely-supremely wonderful monarch the Queen of Hearts wanted to remove it.

'Off with his head!' she'd cried in front of the court, after I had been so wrongly accused of stealing her jam tarts last summer. Her cheeks turned as red as the tarts themselves as she glared at me from her throne.

I did not doubt for a moment that justice would prevail. A thief? Me? Absolutely not. I am the Knave of Hearts! Loyal subject of the royal household. Devoted servant and bearer of the most precious of treasures – the King's crown. I am trustworthy, and I am true. I would not steal a breath from a kitten or a drop of rain from the heaviest of clouds.

Needless to say, the ridiculous trial was over in moments, and the whole matter was forgotten, and my duties continued as they should.

One of my most important responsibilities is to accompany the Queen and King as they take their afternoon tea. Tea is taken in the palace conservatory at three o'clock and consists of:

* twenty-seven egg sandwiches
* nine pots of tea
* five jugs of milk
* three bowls of sugar cubes
* and a giant tiered cake stand containing thirty-one jam tarts

While the royal couple take their tea, I stand beside them holding a crimson velvet cushion bearing a crown.

It is the most important job in the whole of the royal household. A crown must be in the King's presence at all times.

'*But why doesn't he just wear it?*' I hear you ask. This is a very good question and one that has been whispered into my ear by a few brave subjects. If the Queen overheard, her response would most definitely be, 'Off with their heads!'

Well, talking of heads, unfortunately for the King, *his* head is only the size of a small melon. When he wears the precious jewel-encrusted crown (which he *must* do for all state occasions), it slips down over his eyes, and the only way he can see is to tip his chin into the air. This is not a good look for a leader as powerful as the King, so I, the Knave of Hearts, must accompany him throughout the day with a crown upon my crimson cushion.

At tea, the King always serves the Queen. This can make things rather . . . tense, and this afternoon was no exception.

'A cup of tea, my dear?' the King asked Her Majesty as he lifted one of the pots using his two very small hands.

The Queen smiled and nodded, and the King began to pour the tea into her golden cup. Some of it sploshed into the saucer, and her face changed in an instant.

'BE CAREFUL!' she screamed. 'YOU'LL DROWN ME IN TEA!'

The King began to tremble, and the tea splashed everywhere as he placed the pot back on to the table.

I sighed as I stood between them as motionless as possible.

'Milk, my majesty-darling?' said the King.

The Queen smiled and nodded again, but then she snarled as the milk splashed on to the table cloth.

'Six lumps?' said the King, picking up the sugar tongs.

This time, the Queen grabbed the tongs from his hand and pushed him back on to his seat.

'Six lumps? Of course it's six lumps! IT'S ALWAYS SIX LUMPS!' she cried.

The King cowered in his seat.

I watched, holding my breath as the Queen delicately

plopped three sugar lumps into her cup. She struggled to get a hold of the fourth lump with her tongs, and her nostrils began to flare as she snorted like an angry warthog. Her tongue peeped out of the side of her mouth as she concentrated, but she couldn't do it. She screamed in frustration and tossed the tongs high up into the air. The Two of Spades rushed forward, his arms out, ready to catch them. They spun around and around and around, until falling right into his hands. He breathed a huge sigh of relief, then ran back to his position and stood to attention while hiding the tongs behind his back.

This happens every single day at afternoon tea. Last week, the Seven of Diamonds dropped the royal tongs and . . . well . . . let's just say he has been relieved of his duties.

And his head.

The Queen grabbed three more lumps with her sausage-shaped fingers and threw them into her cup with such force that most of the tea splashed up and over into the saucer. She then sat back into her throne with a huff and adjusted her crown. Her head was much larger than the King's, and her crown sat tall and proud.

'STIR!' she snarled through a curled lip.

The King leaped up and began to stir what was left of her tea with a silver spoon.

'Are you looking forward to the Ceremony of the Flamingos later today, my lovely one?' asked the King, his voice wobbling slightly.

The Queen had a great scowl upon her face until she heard the word 'flamingos'.

'Ah . . . the flamingos!' she said, going all soppy. 'Strong necks and straight legs. That's what a croquet mallet needs! Strong necks and straight legs!'

The King clapped his hands together.

'Yes, indeed!' he cried. 'I'm sure there'll be a fantastic selection, my wonderful-ness.'

The Ceremony of the Flamingos happens once a year and is quite a grand affair. A new batch of salmon-pink birds are paraded up and down in front of the royal couple so that they can be assessed for their croquet-mallet potential. The Queen will point to the birds that she wishes to keep in her personal flock. It is an official state occasion, so the King always wears his oversized crown, tipping his head back to see where he is going.

Now, those that are clever among you will have noticed that earlier I said that I accompany the King throughout the day with '*a* spectacular crown' on my cushion and not '*the* spectacular crown'. First, congratulations on your observational skills; and, second, what I am about to tell you could put your own head at risk. When you learn this fact, you must immediately bury it away in the deepest part of your brain, and you are *not* to go digging it up one day and letting it escape out of your mouth. Are we clear on that?

Good.

Then I can tell you this:

The crown that I bear on my cushion is not the real one.

Not in any way, shape or form.

This is because the King once lost the crown. It caused an almighty panic until the Five of Spades found it dangling on a rose bush in the palace garden.

After that, the White Rabbit came up with an idea. 'Why risk losing the real crown when a fake one is perfectly practical?' he said, when he visited one day for afternoon tea.

His nose twitched as he looked at the Queen, waiting for her to reply. She stared at him blankly for a moment, but then she got distracted by the arrival of the jam tarts, grabbing at them with both hands. The rabbit nodded to himself and ticked his 'To Do' list with a swish of his pen:

*   Change His Majesty's real crown for a fake one

And that decided it. For, once the White Rabbit ticked anything on his list, then whatever he ticked would happen. The real crown was hidden away and only used when the King *actually* needed to wear it for state occasions, and the crown that I would bear on my cushion would from that moment on be a worthless fake.

Nobody needed to know.

As the King and Queen continued with their afternoon tea, I looked down at the fake crown on my crimson cushion. My nose slowly curled upwards. The real crown is solid gold, with diamonds around the edge, and a heart at the top, which is encrusted with hundreds of tiny rubies that twinkle in the sunlight. The crown that I now carried on my velvet cushion was made of tin and painted to look like gold. The jewels were made of glass, not diamonds, and the heart at the top was decorated with jam, not rubies. It was a monstrosity.

The Queen of Hearts slurped at her tea and stuffed a jam tart in her mouth as she reached for more. The King had a tart in each hand, while two more bulged in his cheeks. He looked at me and nodded towards the fake crown on my cushion.

'Remember to have my crown ready for the Ceremony of the Flamingos,' he said, showering crumbs everywhere.

A lump of jam slowly made its way down his chin.

'Yes, Your Majesty,' I replied, keeping my gaze lowered, because the King and Queen don't like to be looked at directly. (I also prefer not to see jam tarts being mauled in such a way. I do admire the royal couple in all of their splendidness, but I do wish they would treat the tarts with the respect that they deserve. One should nibble at a jam tart, not stuff.)

'Yes, yes, Knave of Hearts,' piped up the Queen. 'You must do your royal duty well today. The crown must be entirely spectacular!'

I nodded towards her.

'Yes, Your Majesty,' I replied. 'The crown shall be fit for a king.'

The King began to laugh until the Queen slapped her hand on the table and told him to shut up.

When afternoon tea finished, the royal couple rose to retire to their chambers to get ready for the ceremony. I scooted around the vast table to catch up with the King, walking a few paces behind him so that the 'crown' was always close by. He scuttled off down a long corridor and, although he has little legs, I had to trot to keep up with him. His attendants were waiting to greet him, and he quickly turned to me.

'You go and do . . . what you need to be doing . . .' he said, tapping the side of his nose.

The royal couple, the White Rabbit and I are the only ones who know about the crown, and we all need to be discreet. If anyone found out that the crown I carried each day was a fake, there would be an outrage in Wonderland.

'Yes, Your Majesty,' I replied, with a deep bow towards him.

With that, the door to his chamber closed, and I skipped off towards the royal kitchen.

When it had first been decided that the real crown should be replaced with a fake, the big question was where should the real crown be hidden? The palace has plenty of dungeons with armed guards and other protected areas, but I suggested that the best place to hide it should be somewhere a thief wouldn't think to look.

'We need to be clever, Your Majesty,' I had said to the Queen all those months ago. 'We need to be one step ahead of the criminal mind and hide the crown where they would least expect it. How about . . . the royal kitchen?'

The Queen shook her head vigorously.

'No, no, no . . .' she said. 'That's no good. NO GOOD AT ALL!'

She paused for a moment and frowned and tapped her cheek with her finger.

'I've got it!' she cried, making me jump. 'How about . . . the royal kitchen? Yes! That's where it should go!'

I opened my mouth, and then closed it again, quickly nodding. Her Majesty is rather skilled at making all her own decisions.

'What a fine idea,' I replied. 'You are so wise and yet humble in your extremely clever cleverness, ma'am.'

And so it was decided by . . . Her Majesty . . . that the priceless crown should be placed deep within a container filled with flour and hidden at the back of the pantry in the kitchens.

When I got to the royal kitchen, the workers all stopped what they were doing and stood to attention. The staff have a great deal of respect for the authority I have over them.

'I am here on royal duties,' I said loudly. 'I am here to inspect the royal pantry to ensure that the jam tarts are being made using the finest ingredients in all of Wonderland.'

'Of course we're using the finest ingredients, you great nincompoop!' shouted Cook. 'You're just down here tryin' to steal the jam tarts again! Ain't ya?'

The rest of the staff began to laugh. Sometimes they get a bit overexcited and forget how to behave.

'No! No, no!' I shouted above the chatter. 'That is not right at all. I was found completely innocent of that crime. I have never, *ever* stolen any jam tarts ever, ever, ever.'

'Yes 'e 'as!' shouted a pot-washer from the back of the room. ''E's always got jam around his moosh!'

I instinctively wiped at my mouth with my sleeve, and the laughing got louder.

'Look at 'im! 'E's trying to hide the evidence!' called the pastry chef from under his puffy white hat. ''E finks we're as fick as the Queen!'

Everyone fell into deathly silence as they stared at the pastry chef. They blinked at each other, waiting for a screeching voice to cry, '*Off with his head!*' but, after a few moments, there was no shout, and everyone relaxed.

'I am not a thief, and I am not stealing the jam tarts!' I cried. 'I am here on official royal duties, and you should all get back to your posts immediately, or I shall . . . I shall . . . I shall become very angry indeed!'

I stamped my foot, and the crown fell off the cushion and on to the floor with a clatter.

'Look at 'im!' said Cook. ''E can't even keep the crown on 'is cushion!'

I quickly picked it up, relieved it was not the real one.

'Get back to your work!' I shouted, with a quite impressive amount of firmness. 'If you don't, I will tell the Queen about you, and your heads will all come off! Every single one!'

'Well, that ain't gonna 'appen,' said a small, weedy woman, who began to spoon great dollops of jam into tart cases. 'The Queen ain't gonna want to risk losing us and not 'aving any afternoon tea, is she?'

The rest of the group grumbled in agreement, but they each turned back to their work. There is no doubting my authority here. They all realize how superior I am to them, and they always treat me with a great deal of respect.

While they were busy, I headed to the pantry – a great big cupboard with five large shelves. This is where the flour, sugar, eggs and jam are kept. I put my cushion down, stood on my tiptoes and reached for a jar of flour hidden at the back on the very top shelf. It was heavy, and I needed two hands to ease it out and on to the floor. I prised the lid off and pushed my fingers into the soft flour. They immediately felt something cold and hard. The crown! I carefully pulled it out and shook the flour off. The heart at the top, which was decorated with rubies, glistened in the daylight. The row of precious diamonds twinkled as I blew the white flour off them. It truly was spectacular. I took the fake crown and stuffed it into the jar, scooping flour over the top to hide it from view, and placed the real crown on top of my cushion. Then, straightening my back and pointing my nose into the air, I left the kitchens.

The Ceremony of the Flamingos was a splendid occasion. As usual, the Queen insisted that the birds parade up and down, up and down, and she clapped her hands and grinned as she pointed to those she wanted for her flock. Eventually there was just one bird left. Its feathers were sticking out all over the place, and its beak was crooked. As it walked, it swayed its head from side to side like it was listening to music that only it could hear. The Queen clapped her hands again and pointed towards the bird.

'And I'll have that one too!' she said. 'Yes! I definitely want that one!'

She was supposed to choose the best birds for her flock, but she always picked every single one.

The ceremony had gone on for hours, and the King had fallen asleep on his throne, the royal crown slipping down over his eyes as he slumped further and further into his chair.

'WAKE UP, KING!' cried the Queen.

He jolted upright, and the crown dropped down round his neck like a ring round a coconut. I rushed over with the cushion and presented it to him, ready to receive the crown. He eased the crown up over his little head, and then huffed as he plonked it down on to the cushion.

'Pesky thing!' he said. 'Take it back, Knave!'

I bowed deeply as he got up, and then I quickly trotted across the lawns towards the palace.

It was a puzzle to me that he couldn't see the beauty in the crown. It was a thing of wonder, of amazing workmanship, and it was – of course – incredibly valuable. The kind of valuable that could change a life forever.

I returned with the crown to the kitchens. The cook was the only person there now, and she looked up at me with a grunt and a huff but didn't say anything.

I went to the pantry and took down the jar with the flour and removed the fake crown. It looked so dull and pathetic to my eyes. Was I the only one who appreciated the beauty of the real crown? I sighed, put the jar back on to the shelf and headed back to my quarters.

My room is plain but good enough for my needs. In it, I have a bed, a chair, a wardrobe and a suitcase.

I am the Knave of Hearts, and my heart was truly pounding in my chest as I looked around my room and thought about what I was about to do. I took a deep breath, then reached for my suitcase from underneath my bed and opened it up. I went to my wardrobe, removed my clothes, folded them and placed them in a neat pile inside the case. Then, tossing the dented fake crown on to my bed, I picked up the crimson cushion and placed it on top of my clothes.

It was such a plain, simple cushion that had accompanied me on all of my duties, but it also had a hidden secret. While I had been alone in my room in the quiet evenings, I had 'improved' the cushion with the use of a needle and cotton.

Hidden on the underside of the cushion was a pocket. A pocket that I have stitched with absolute precision – each stitch so tiny it can barely be seen, even by the most curious of eyes.

A pocket that has been so effective for making things 'disappear'.

Like jam tarts, for instance.

I've stolen at least three hundred now, enjoying their delicious jamminess within the privacy of my room and eating them with the delicacy and refinement they deserve. The trial was a bit of an inconvenience, but fortunately that strange girl Alice decided to grow as large as a house right there in the court. In the chaos that followed, the charges against me were all forgotten.

I slid my hand inside the secret pocket of the cushion and took out the crown. The *real* crown with its rubies and diamonds.

'You're coming with me,' I said, swallowing as I stared at the exquisite twinkling gems. A jam-tart thief? How boring that seemed now. I hid the crown back inside the cushion and closed my suitcase with a click and a clunk.

I turned and faced my room for one last time and then opened my door.

Will I lose my head? I doubt it. By the time the Queen realizes I have stolen the King's crown, I will have reached the edge of Wonderland and arrived at the sea. They will spend days searching the palace grounds before they even *think* about looking further. I'd been surrounded by idiots for so long. I couldn't wait to escape their dull, tiny brains.

I closed my door and sneaked through the dark shadows of the corridors until I emerged on to the palace steps. I ran across the moonlit forecourt and past the guard snoring into his belly.

As I skipped down the road with my case, I grinned to myself. I'd never seen the ocean before, and I was excited to hear the roar of the waves. What excitement would be waiting for me there, I wondered? I'd heard there was a rather murderous Walrus who lived by the sea, and I couldn't wait to meet him. I think that maybe we could be friends.

How the Cheshire Cat
Got His Smile

by Piers Torday

Like millions of children before and after me, I was captivated by the surreal, hilarious and occasionally alarming madness of Lewis Carroll's Wonderland when I first encountered it, my already overactive young imagination aided by John Tenniel's classic illustrations. But of all the many talking, singing and downright peculiar creatures to be discovered down the rabbit hole, none intrigued me more than the Cheshire Cat.

Wonderland can seem frenetic, with dashing rabbits, arguing playing cards, people changing size all the time – and this enigmatic, eerily grinning oversized cat draped over a branch perplexed me. Where had he come from? Why was he almost more smile than cat? Some say the phrase to 'grin like a Cheshire Cat' comes from cats delighting at the abundance of milk and cream to be found in dairy rich Cheshire, others that Carroll found inspiration in an old church carving. But I had a rather different idea . . .

Piers Torday

The first mistake Doctor Aziz made was to open the door. The second was to look down. For there, by the light of his lantern, was a small kitten curled up on the doorstep, mewling fit to wake the entire river bank. A short-haired tabby, with an uncommonly long tail.

'Well, well. A surprise gift! Let us see what my little Duchess makes of you.' He rested the lantern on the floor, and, pulling on his smart kid gloves, scooped up the poor kitty, marched straight back indoors and presented it to his frowning daughter.

The little Duchess, or Mary Anne (to give his daughter her correct name), wrinkled her nose. Another mouth to feed was the last thing she needed. She was hard pressed as it was keeping their curious old home, Glasshouses, from looking back to front all the time. It was nestled deep in some tangled woods on a forgotten, overgrown edge of the River Thames, and was named Glasshouses for its preponderance of windows in the strangest places, and mirrors in the darkest corners.

Mary Anne truly thought she had the worst of jobs. While her father got to spend hours hidden behind tottering piles of paper in his study, she was expected keep the multiple windows and mirrors of the house sparkling clean, not to mention preparing the meals, sweeping the floor, washing his clothes . . .

Life had not always been so, of course.

Her parents, Doctor Abdul Aziz and her late mother, the much-missed Mrs Rose Sedley Aziz, had met in India before Mary Anne was born. Political causes had brought the ever-campaigning Mrs Aziz back to England, her scientist husband in tow. Shortly after their arrival at Glasshouses, their one and only daughter had been born.

What a blissful childhood it had been! The long games of chess with her father in his study, while he puffed away on his beloved hookah pipe. Walks by the river, games of cards on rainy days, her mother teaching her how to bake pastries in the kitchen . . . Mary Anne's eyes misted up at the memory, and she had to turn away.

'What is it, my little Duchess?'

'Nothing, Father,' she lied.

Nothing, in a way, had been the cause of it all. Or next to nothing, in the shape of a humble fly. An insect that had visited her mother one summer night and left its red mark upon her skin. A fly that her scientist father had observed upon her and left unharmed. For this gentle soul of a man had often been described as someone who 'wouldn't hurt a fly'.

The kind-hearted Doctor had taken this description as

an instruction, an ideal to live up to so long as he lived. But the fly had no such honour, no compunction in harming the Doctor's wife.

Its bite contained the seed of a mysterious fever, which grew and grew, resisting all draughts and ointments, until it swallowed Mary Anne's mother clean up, lost forever. Her father, lost in grief, mused obsessively on his decision not to hurt the fly in the first place.

'*No one*,' he swore in his diary, '*will ever make the same mistake with the English language again.*'

For Doctor Aziz did not blame himself for his wife's death. He certainly did not blame his wife, and he did not even blame the fly. He took issue with the English language itself. It never *actually* rained cats and dogs. Not one farmer of his acquaintance counted their chickens before their eggs were hatched. And which hunter yet born had developed the skill to kill two birds with one stone?

If he, the great Doctor Aziz, did not act now, then further tragedy was inevitable! The risk for misunderstandings such as this was too great. He would save the English language from itself, through the only means available to him:

Science.

Clear-headed, logical, rational experiments would rid

the country of these dangerous colloquialisms. Once everyone saw the evidence, they would mend their ways. No one needed to pay for anything with an arm or a leg ever again.

So he began work on his greatest ever experiment, the experiment that would take over their lives and their home, the experiment after which *nothing* would ever be the same again.

Doctor Aziz filled Glasshouses with animals, beginning with a hare. Standing at the end of his long, flower-filled garden, studying his pocket watch, he set the creature to racing with a tortoise up and down the lawn, to see whether slow and steady *did* win the race. It didn't.

Then the Doctor spent a very long time persuading a white rabbit to climb into his top hat, to see if pulling him out was as easy and as magical a solution as people so frequently suggested.

'A solution to what?' Mary Anne had asked.

'I won't know till I try,' said Doctor Aziz, gripping the poor creature by its ears as he tried, in vain, to persuade him to leave the warm shadows of the hat.

There seemed to be a new arrival every day. Could a bird in the hand truly be worth two in the bush? Doctor Aziz unwisely tried to find out with a pigeon and a couple of ducks, with predictably noisy results.

But as Mary Anne patiently bandaged up his pecked hand, the Doctor was already planning his next scientific test of popular proverbs. Later that afternoon, he wrote to London Zoo to ask if he could borrow three of their brightest and pinkest flamingos. Arriving on a horse and cart the next week, they were installed on the Doctor's beloved croquet lawn that same evening, while he lay in wait, out of sight, with a pair of binoculars and a notebook to see if the 'early bird really did catch the worm'.

'Being bright pink, as they are, there is no chance of me missing them,' he explained to his baffled daughter. (The fact that flamingos of course only eat fish, rather than worms, seemed to have escaped his attention.)

Then a bright-eyed puppy arrived one afternoon, panting and wagging its tail, only to be knocked out immediately with a sleeping draught. Doctor Aziz carefully laid the slumbering pup out right at the top of the stairs, just as Mary Anne approached with a tottering tea tray piled high with cups, saucers and a cake stand.

Writing up his notes later, the Doctor remarked, 'In conclusion, we should *not* let sleeping dogs lie. Mary Anne is in most firm agreement on this point.'

'Exactly so,' said Mary Anne, grimacing and wondering

when this madness would end. But by the time she had tidied up the broken tea things, her father was standing on a chair, heaving a glass cabinet off a case housing a carefully stuffed dodo.

'Now, let's see how dead you truly are,' he said, a syringe of adrenaline clamped between his teeth, as he rolled up his sleeves.

It was into this madhouse of zoological and proverbial experimentation that the innocent and ill-fated cat had wandered.

'You're just another mouth to feed – I hope you know that. You must work for your supper around here. We have a problem. Lots of little problems with tails, in fact.' Mary Anne glared angrily at the Doctor, who looked at his polished shoes in shame.

'The mice, I assume,' he said.

'Yes, the mice!' she said.

'But what about my test? I have a particularly good phrase lined up for our new feline friend. For they say that—'

'The mice, Father!' Mary Anne said again.

One of the Doctor's more bizarre recent installations (even by his standards) was a doll's house populated entirely by mice. It had all the usual accoutrements (carefully made model beds and cupboards; tables covered in crockery), as well as several very unusual additions (miniature tennis rackets and balls, a tiny chess set, packs of cards, a dressing-up box and even a doll's-house-sized piano).

'You see,' Doctor Aziz had said, carefully lowering the piano into the first floor of the house, where a rodent waited with open arms to chew it to pieces, 'I simply must find out whether when the cat's away—'

'The mice will play?' Mary Anne had said in disbelief. 'Out of your head, is what you are. Out of your head!'

As she feared, the mice had only played in one way. There were holes in the skirting board, droppings on the rugs, and barely a morsel of food in the larder left untouched by their little inquisitive teeth.

But at last, here was an animal arrival to Glasshouses who might be put to some practical use.

'Can I keep this one, Father?' she implored. 'Can't he just be a normal cat that might actually be some use around this madhouse of ours?'

'Oh, but don't you see, my dear Mary Anne, he will be of the greatest use.' Doctor Aziz peered through his glasses at the tiny kitten, who stared straight back in grumpy bewilderment. 'He will be of use to science. For I intend to study this feline and find out, once and for all, whether—'

Mary Anne shook her head in a way that brooked no further discussion.

'The only thing this poor little mite is going to find out is what's good for him. Beginning with a saucer of milk in the kitchen! Now be off with you, Father, and back to your flamingos or dodo, or whatever it is now, before I really lose my temper!'

With that, she whisked the young kitten off, leaving Doctor Aziz standing speechless in the hall, marvelling at how much his only daughter reminded him of his late wife.

Mary Anne slung an old blanket over an armchair by the fire for the kitten's bed and gave him balls of wool to play with. Day by day, the kitten's fur grew less patchy, and his meows less strident. He began to explore his new home and enjoyed curling up on the Doctor's lap of an evening, as his master perused his latest volume of scientific research (a very boring one, without any pictures, the puss noted).

Brewer's Phrase and Fable, read the cat silently to itself, because this cat was remarkably inquisitive, a fact that neither Doctor Aziz nor Mary Anne had bothered to discover for themselves.

'You are a very affectionate creature,' remarked the

Doctor. 'I wonder what we should call him, my dear?'

'Mousecatcher, if I have anything to do with it,' said Mary Anne, inspecting a lump of Cheddar cheese on her plate, which more resembled Swiss cheese, on account of the holes in it.

'A most curious thing, though,' noted Doctor Aziz, as he stroked the ball of fur on his lap. 'This cat does not purr.'

'You're probably just stroking him the wrong way.'

'But have you not observed, dear child? He never purrs. Not when he dozes in the sun. Not after supping from one of your saucers of milk. Not even after a dozen gentle strokes.'

The cat sat comfortably but silently on his lap, keeping his thoughts on the matter to himself, as cats like to do.

'Give him a chance – he's only small.'

'I wonder if he even smiles?'

'Cats don't smile!' declared Mary Anne, taking a large bite of her hole-ridden Cheddar.

'This one certainly doesn't. Perhaps a name would help. A name for a cat that doesn't smile.' He tickled the scruff of the creature's neck. But the cat didn't close his eyes or purr, or make the approximation of a human smile that other cats did.

'Cheshire!' said Mary Anne suddenly.

'Excuse me?'

'Cheshire!' she said again. 'Great Aunt Agatha lives in Cheshire, and she never smiles. Ever.'

'Indeed she doesn't!' crowed Doctor Aziz with approval. His late wife's great-aunt was not inclined to jollity of any kind. 'Perhaps she and the cat are related?'

And that settled it. Cheshire the Cat it was.

He twisted himself between their legs, tail flicking this way and that.

'Now you are named, you must start earning your keep,' said Mary Ann, tickling him behind the ears.

For the Doctor's mice were now running rampant throughout the house, chewing their way through parcels of cheese, sacks of grain and loaves of bread as if there was a war on. (There wasn't. At least, not one involving mice.)

But Cheshire was not interested in catching things.

Like the Doctor, he had only one approach to the world around him.

He was curious.

It was true, he did not have the training of Doctor Aziz, his years of experience, knowledge and books. Cheshire had no study or laboratory. He was entirely oblivious to the principles of fieldwork, and he could no more write a detailed report for the Royal Society than he could boil an egg.

However, he did not need to.

For when it came to the scientific study of animals, Cheshire had one crucial advantage.

He was one.

Under a tree in front of the house lay the hutch where Doctor Aziz kept his racing hare. The tortoise lived in a crate under some lettuce leaves next to it. Cheshire simply strolled across the lawn and tapped sharply on the hare's hutch door with his claw.

'Excuse me, Hare,' he said, in that voice only other animals can understand. 'I am curious. Why do you always beat the tortoise in a race when the stories suggest otherwise?'

'Because he cheats!' piped up the tortoise from under his lettuce leaf.

'I wasn't talking to you,' said Cheshire. 'Hare, why do you win?'

The hare sidled up to the cage door, his eyes rolling, his lips pulled back over his teeth in a crazed grin. Cheshire took a step back. The poor creature was clearly insane, perhaps driven so by his endless unnecessary races against an irritable tortoise.

'Which month is it?' asked Cheshire suspiciously.

'March!' said the hare, pretending to box an imaginary opponent.

'That settles it,' said Cheshire. 'You must be mad. Mad as a—'

'Hatter?' said the hare.

'Something like that. Now, curious as I am, I have another question for you, March Hare. Between a cat and a hare, who would win that race?'

'Why do you want to know, Cat?'

'Let's just say . . . I wish to study the world. I am curious!'

'It is not a good idea for cats to be curious.'

'There is only one way to find out if you are right,' said Cheshire, and he hooked the catch of the hutch with his claw.

The March Hare bounded out, and within seconds Cheshire was fast on his tail. They raced all over the garden, the hare frantically looking for a means of escape. But the fast-flowing river at the end of the garden, and the dark, tangled woods on either side, did not offer any. Then, just as Cheshire was about to pounce on the hare, at the last minute, his prey disappeared into the wall of thorny briars that divided the lawn and the wild wood and did not reappear.

'Come out – the race is not yet over!' the cat called after the hare, but to no avail.

Cheshire skulked back to the house in disappointment, his frown deeper than ever before. As he did so, Cheshire noticed the white rabbit with pink eyes peering at him out of his top hat.

'What are you looking at?' he snarled.

'Oh dear! Oh dear!' said the rabbit. 'Please don't eat me!'

'I shall have to catch you first,' said Cheshire, and pushed the top hat over with his paw. The white rabbit leaped out, bounding as fast as he could for the wood, charging into the prickly briars.

'Curiouser and curiouser,' said Cheshire to himself.

Next, he asked the pigeons and the ducks whether if he ate a pigeon, that would make a bird in the stomach worth two in the pond, and they also fled for the thorny wood. One by one, creature by creature, he drove all the members of the Doctor's menagerie away and into the woods.

He pulled a feather out of his mouth and picked some fur from his claw. Well, it was true, he had not fully satisfied his curiosity, but . . . it had been fun, hadn't it?

Cheshire experienced a lovely new feeling.

A feeling that—

'CHESHIRE!'

It was not so much a cry, as a scream of desolation. Doctor Aziz and Mary Anne had returned from their afternoon's excursion and were standing at the edge of the garden, coats over their arms, barely able to take in the scene of devastation – the upturned hutch, the shredded top hat, the churned-up lawn . . .

'What *have* you done, you wretched animal?'

The normally mild-mannered Doctor Aziz took all leave of his senses and lunged for Cheshire, who – understandably – ran away, round the side of the house. Followed by a remonstrating Mary Ann, pleading for calm, the Doctor chased him through the parlour. Cheshire knocked over the hookah and got tangled in the pipe, dragging it with him. He bolted into the dining room and crashed straight into an occasional table holding a plate of jam tarts Mary Anne had prepared earlier for their tea, which tipped on to the cat's back in an explosion of pastry crumbs and jam.

Suddenly, it looked like the saying was right after all.

Curiosity *was* going to kill the cat.

Sticky with fruit, still dragging the hookah behind him, yowling for his life as the Doctor roared not far behind, Cheshire hurtled through the drawing room, scattering a pile of playing cards that flew into the air before showering down on to the cat's jam-covered back, as he smashed through the French windows and out into the garden again.

The late evening shadows lengthened towards the river in darkening stripes. Cheshire was foolhardy but not foolish – cats could not swim. There was only one way out.

Cheshire tore into the brambles and disappeared.

Doctor Aziz and his daughter tried to follow him, but the thorns were too thick and sharp. Mary Anne looked up at her father, distraught. They had lost another life. Several lives.

'It's no good, Father – he's gone. Like all the others.'

Her father was not distraught. He was already scribbling in his notebook with approval. 'At last! I have proved a great saying correct, finally. My wife's memory will not be in vain. The world *is* as we understand it to be. Curiosity *did* kill the cat, after all!'

But in fact, far on the other side of the hedge, which ran for several miles along the river bank, Cheshire the Cat stood by a tree, the hookah pipe still wrapped around his legs, cards and jam still plastered to his fur, and very much alive. He was looking at the bottom of the tree, where there was an enormous black hole.

He peered into the hole, whiskers twitching.

From far down below, he could hear the strangest sound.

A song, calling up to him, sung by a choir of animal voices . . .

Thus grew the tale of Wonderland:
Thus, slowly, one by one . . .

'Wonderland?' said Cheshire to himself. 'What a curious name!'

He touched his fur with a paw, licking the jam. A Queen of Hearts playing card was stuck to his leg. What a picture he must be! He marvelled at the nonsense that had brought him here. None of it made any sense. Not a single word.

As he realized this, he released something held deep inside. The feeling he had felt before the Doctor caught him bubbled up uncontrollably. It stretched his mouth, pulled at his eyebrows, snorted air through his nose, and . . . Cheshire the Cat began to smile. He began to smile more and more, till the grin stretched right across his face like a slice of moon in an autumn sky.

The more he began to grin, the more he chuckled . . .

and then guffawed. He guffawed so much that he rocked from side to side, and he rocked so much that he tipped clean over into the hole . . . and started to fall . . . and he kept on smiling all the way down to the bottom.

And there he remained, where he is still smiling to this very day, if you are ever brave enough to go looking for him.

The Caterpillar and the Moth Rumour

by Amy Wilson

I grew up with Alice; my grandparents gave me her adventures when I was five, and I loved them dearly, have kept them with me through all the years, and shared them with my own children.

It's a huge honour to have been asked to write this story, but, also, such a joy! The love I felt for the Caterpillar by the time we finished our own adventure together was a gift I hadn't expected. He now sits on his mushroom in a very special place in my heart.

Amy Wilson

Deep down in the dark they call to me, my brothers and sisters. In my dreams, they flutter about me, petals blown here and there at the whim of the wind. They laugh as they swirl, and their voices are still children's voices.

When I wake, their laughter continues to ring in my ears, but the joy of the dream is long gone.

'Caterpillar?'

Nobody knows my true name here. I left it behind when I came to Wonderland. It was a new start, and I brought nothing but myself and the magic, which grew here until it was a sparking, rolling cloud around my body.

'Caterpillar, I've come to tell you. There is trouble among the tulips,' says the Dormouse.

'The trouble with tulips,' I say, poking my head through the cloud, 'is that their heads are too big for their stems.'

'That may be,' the Dormouse says, shifting his weight, twisting a whisker with a shaking paw. 'But . . .'

'But? Why does a but need to come into it?'

'They are whispering, my dear Caterpillar. Of change to come.'

I stare at him. That dream lingers in my mind. A flutter of wings, the spin and tumble through the air.

'They say . . .' The Dormouse blinks his shining black

eyes, and his upper lip curls. 'They say there is a dread moth . . .'

Magic funnels up over my head. I take a breath and, with a great deal of effort, put the whole cloud behind me. *No.*

Not here. Not now. This is my place. This is my mushroom, pale and smooth. This is my clearing, where the beech and the oak trees stand sentry. Where the thistles and buttercups and the tall green blades of grass gather to hear my wisdom.

Along with the rest of Wonderland.

'No more of this chitty-chatty,' I tell him. 'The mushroom is OPEN.'

My voice fills the clearing, and the trees carry my words up high, and the birds call them over the rest of Wonderland.

And they come, from far and wide. They come with their troubles and their wishes. They lollop, lope, march, crawl, prance, and there they stand, before my mushroom: the White Rabbit, the Carpenter, the Mad Hatter, the Queen of Hearts herself. They all need my magic: to keep a hankie white, to grow a little wisdom, to make the tea pour *out* of the teapot rather than *in*, to hide the jam tarts from the marauding Queen of Spades.

I sit and listen, and their troubles fill my mind and quiet the whispers of the night. I busy myself dishing out bits of mushroom, enchanted by my magic. This is my life, and it is the life I wanted, but I've noticed something. Every time I do this, my cloud gets thicker. Every moment of every day, it roils heavier about my body, until sometimes I'm hardly there at all. My visitors must speak to a shifting, shimmering cloud of sparkles with a foot poking out. Or, if they're lucky, an eye.

Today, the clearing around my mushroom carries the bite of a chill. Leaves have begun to fall, autumn is on its way and the hint of change has made everybody impatient. I let the cloud swirl up around me, for I know how it glints in the early morning light, how it billows and makes a show of me. By the time I look up, the queue to the mushroom is several yards long.

Naturally, the Queen's voice, as she arrives at the end of the queue, is the most insistent.

'I must see him at once!' she cries, drawing a spotted umbrella from her voluminous skirts. 'Clear the path! Out of my way!' And so she continues, charging with her head down, brolly sweeping hither and thither until she is standing before me, out of breath and quite pink in the cheeks.

'Ye-es?' I ask.

'I must speak with you immediately!' she demands.

'And so you are,' I say. 'Was that all?'

'Was what all?'

'You said you must speak with me immediately, and so you have. Do you need anything else?'

I give her a smile.

'No! I mean yes! Confounded creature,' the Queen mutters, before taking a deep breath and pasting a smile across her face. 'I need your help, if you would.'

'Would I?'

There's a titter. The Queen turns and waves her brolly at the crowd behind her. 'Get back!' she commands. 'This is a private matter!'

'You pushed in!' shouts an oyster.

'I am your Queen! I am here on urgent state business!'

'Well, you are in a state, but there's nothing new about that!' comes another voice, a grinning, feline sort of a voice, from deep within the safety of the crowd.

The Queen marches down the queue, which curls into the shape of a question mark, and her eyes blaze as she looks for the culprit. Clouds roll over the sun, and even the trees draw in, but the crowd is silent. Eventually she growls under her breath and marches back to me.

'Well?' she demands.

'The more I give, the more there is.' I sigh. 'Just look at it all.' I wave a foot through the dazzling, whirling storm of my magic. 'Soon I shan't be able to escape it at all.'

'That is *your* problem,' says the Queen, wrinkling her nose and stabbing the needle-point of the brolly into the grass. 'I need you to help me with *mine*!'

'And what *is* your problem?'

'The roses are being difficult,' she says. 'I chopped off their heads, and they absolutely refuse to grow new ones.'

'Why did you chop off their heads?'

'They went pink!'

'And what colour do you expect them to be?'

'RED, OF COURSE,' she roars. 'But the colour won't stay, no matter how many times we paint them.'

'Let them be whatever colour they *are*, I should say.'

'Oh, you should, should you?'

'Or do you prefer the bare *stalks*?'

'No,' she snaps.

I reach out a hand to very edge of the mushroom. The magic around me unravels, and one small section turns to rainbow colours that shimmer and shift. The sun breaks free of the clouds overhead, and the trees send down a scatter of leaves as they settle back. I break off the enchanted piece of mushroom and hand it to the Queen.

'They will be what they will be,' I warn her in my best sing-song voice.

She shows me her teeth in not-a-smile-at-all and stalks off.

The Mad Hatter steps forward. He takes off his hat, holds it to his chest and winks at me.

'What do you need?'

'Only to tell you what you already know.'

'Be quick about it, then,' I snap.

'Change is coming,' he crows. 'We have all seen it. The *dread wolf moth* is here, and it calls for *killing*!'

A wave of chatter breaks out through the queue. Wings flutter, out of sight.

'No more!' I shout. 'No more magic today!'

There's a loud groan.

'Blame the Hatter! Now off! Off with you all!'

I retreat to the safety of my cloud until the clearing is quiet and still. Except for the infernal Dormouse. He folds his arms as he considers me.

'We must construct a sign,' I tell him.

'And what are we signing?'

'We-lllll,' I ponder aloud. 'CLOSED FOR BUSINESS.'

'That *is* a sign,' says the Dormouse. 'A sign of trouble, I'd say.'

'Oh, *you'd* say, would you?' I demand. 'And who are *you* to say such?'

'A friend? Or, at the least, an accomplice,' he says, with a furry sort of shrug.

'Well then, accomplice, why don't you sign me a sign?'

'Are you going to investigate the *dread wolf moth*?' His nose twitches. Mouse he may be, but oh how he hankers for adventure. 'The Hatter did not lie, you know. As I was *trying* to tell you earlier, there have indeed been rumours of this moth. Down in the deep dark, beyond the old yew. They say its presence will bring change.'

'No!' I say. '*They* are wrong. *They* always are. Where did this rumour come from?'

'The grass and the trees, and the worms that dig the soil. The birds that eat the worms, and the fox that chases the birds.'

'Does he catch them?'

'Not yet. He is only young.'

'And yet you take his word?'

'Better that than his sharp teeth! He says the creature casts a shadow over all it touches, and it calls for *killing, killing*!'

The clover and the trees and the buttercups all are silent, the clearing completely still. I retreat into my magic cloud, but it itches at my skin, and the memories come bright as stars in a clear sky. Memories of the time before I was here, of a place far away. Of a life without this magic, without this cloud, or this mushroom. Of the thing that loomed over all of us. The thing I ran away from.

I shiver.

No.

But the Dormouse is waiting. He has found a sheet of yellow parchment, a quill and a bottle of deepest nightshade ink. I write the words, and they curl and spark with magic. The sign, once complete, is hung with a silver chain over the tattered edges of the mushroom.

Closed for Business.

'What now?' demands the Dormouse.

'No more advice. No more magic. I am going to Have A Rest.'

'But the moth!'

'No! No to moths. No to *you*, dear Dormouse.'

There's a long silence. The woodland is listening. Every flower, tree, every creature. A golden leaf flutters to the ground. The Dormouse watches it, his black eyes deep in thought.

'I will come with you to investigate,' he says eventually, thrusting out his tiny whiskered chin.

'*You?*' I laugh. 'Who are *you?*'

'I am a mouse,' says the Dormouse. 'The question is, who are *you?*'

'CLOSED FOR BUSINESS,' I roar, pulling my cloud around me.

Sleep doesn't come easily. The cloud clings and sparkles at my knees and scratches at my neck. The more I struggle against it, the more it crackles. By the time the birds start to sing of the new day, I know.

There's no more hiding.

There's no more putting it off.

Word of the moth has awoken the thing inside me that was always there. The magic is out of control, and the only answer is to confront it.

I eat a few golden leaves, taste the bite of winter in their veins, and when I emerge from my cloud, there is the Dormouse, still waiting, just as I knew he would be.

It is time.

It's a twisty, tangly way through the murk of the wood. The sun does not reach this part of the world, and the stream is a dark ribbon that winds from tree to tree. Dormouse is singing *fala-la-di-da* rather tunefully, but that's no help whatsoever.

'Please do stop,' I burst out eventually, as we reach the yew tree.

'*La-oh!*' The Dormouse breaks off. 'Yes. Perhaps a more adventuresome sort of ditty.' And off he goes in a lower, more important sort of voice: '*The woods they are a-trembling, but not the heroes-OH! The skies may be a-weeping, but we shall keep a-going-OH!*'

'No!' I say. 'Now, where was this rumour begun? Who spoke it first?'

'They say it was the Cheshire Cat,' says the Dormouse with a yawn, after a long and rather awkward pause.

I stop. 'What?'

'He whispered of the worms and the roots and the . . . Oh dear, what was the order?'

'*The grass and the trees, and the worms that dig the soil. The birds that eat the worms, and the fox that chases the birds*,' comes a familiar, mocking sort of voice.

The Cheshire Cat.

The Dormouse gives a squeak of fear and disappears off into the undergrowth.

'Well, aren't you a little travelling cloud of adventure?'

the cat says with a grin, leaping down from the branches of the yew.

'What is this nonsense?' I demand, making myself larger to match his size. 'It was you who made up that natty rhyme, and so now you have tricked me here, for what?'

'It is no trick, my dear. It is the dread wolf moth . . . It calls for killing, and it casts its shadow, and all the silly creatures flee.'

'Have you seen it?'

'Naturally.'

'And?'

'And what?'

'And what say you?'

'I say it is none of my business whatsoever. The question, dear Caterpillar –' the Cheshire Cat gives another of his slow, wide grins and begins to lick one of his front paws, claws glinting in the gloom – 'is what it has to do with *you*, and whether you will stop hiding in that cloud of yours to find out!'

'Where is this creature?' I ask as the cloud spirals out over my head. By the time I've got it under control, the Cheshire Cat is gone, and only that malevolent feline grin lingers in my mind.

Well. Then it is up to me. I make my way along the dirt path that winds between the trees, and as I go I let my size diminish, until I'm back to the perfect height of three and a half inches.

And then I'm in a new part of the forest, and the change is clear to see. The sun steals in through the branches of the ancient oak trees, and tiny golden flowers grow between the feet of those giants, nodding their sweet heads at me. I take a breath of that clear, sun-filled air, and it tastes good. The grass is green; the sky is blue. In the distance, birds sing.

My magic begins to itch, and darkness falls over me with fluttering wings and whispered song that *sounds* like *killing* but isn't. I look up as the shadow of the creature looms larger and larger, and the golden flowers curl their petals, shrinking into the comfort of the sturdy oaks, as the birdsong drifts away. I wish I'd remained larger. I wish the cloud of magic was a wall that nobody could penetrate. I wish I'd never left the mushroom. I wish for the Queen's screeching voice, for the gentle shiver of the Dormouse's upper lip.

My past has come to find me.

Before I came to Wonderland, change had been coming. I saw it in my sisters and my brothers. In all of our friends.

And I didn't like it.

I didn't like their disappearance into private homes. I didn't like their fluttering wings when they emerged as butterflies. We were caterpillars, we always had been, and that was only right.

When the last of my sisters drew her home around her and shut herself away, I left. Marched on my fine furry caterpillar legs into Wonderland, where anything was possible, and the beginnings of my home became the shifting cloud of magic.

Which grew, and grew, and itched, and nearly overcame me.

The dread wolf moth is no moth. And it does not shout for *killing*.

It is my sister, Cassandra. And she is looking for me.

'Colin!' she calls. 'Here you are! Oh, we've been so worried – how could you leave us for so long? How are you still a caterpillar? What is this that sparks and rolls over you? Isn't it very uncomfortable?'

She always did talk a lot.

'Why won't you let your wings come? Why are you hiding here?'

'I am not hiding here,' I say with a sniff, tucking the cloud behind me with a twist of feet and a great deal of willpower. 'I have a role. I am an advisor to royalty! All in Wonderland have heard of me, and I use my magic with great wisdom.'

She laughs. Her wings shiver constantly, and they are, now that I can see more closely, very beautiful. Black with a white streak.

'What have you become?' I demand.

'A white admiral.'

'They call you the dread wolf moth. You have brought terror with your flittering wings and your shouts of *killing*!'

'Nonsense,' she says. 'I found the bramble, and the nectar was wonderful, and so I stayed, and the longer I stayed, the more I felt your presence. I was calling for you, *Colin*!'

'Yes.' I sigh. 'I suppose you were.'

I let the cloud of magic waft free once more, and it twines about my body.

'Just let it happen, dear brother,' says Cassie, her voice more gentle. 'You will do wonderful things with wings, as well as without them. You can be wise, you can still advise, but also you can *fly*! Have adventure, see the dawn from the sky, meet the stars as they fill the night. You can be with me, and with our brothers and sisters. It is a wonderful thing, to be a butterfly!'

'I don't like it,' I say, hearing the petulance in my voice.

'You have never tried it,' she says. 'If this place, Wonderland, is the place where anything can happen, then this should happen too.'

'And if I still don't like it?'

'You will still be you. You will be you, with wings. There is nothing not to like.'

'I don't like change.'

'Pah,' she says. 'Change will come, whether you like it or not. Even now your home is calling. How can you impart wisdom when you refuse to be true to yourself?'

Deep within the cloud, I stick out my tongue. The magic tastes of bright new things. Of moonshine, and dew on cobwebs; of the rush of spring water, of the morning haze over a green field.

Perhaps I could see more of it all.

If I were a butterfly.

The magic senses a chink in my armour and snuggles in. I stare at the bright wisps of possibility, of unknown things. Catch my sister's eye.

'You'll be here when I am new again?'

'I'll be here all along,' she says.

*

It is dawn. I can tell from the birdsong, and the glow of pink light between the trees, the roll of fog still upon the grass. I cling to a twig, my body scrunched and small and stiff.

What is this nonsense? I wonder.

And then I remember.

There is no cloud of magic now. It is inside me. Inside the wings that

s t r e t c h

and shiver

and kiss the clear, cool air.

'Are you ready?' asks my sister, as she flutters down to meet me.

I am unsteady and new.

I am a *butterfly*.

And the world is full of wonder.

We take to the skies, and we tumble and dance and laugh.

And there is the dear Dormouse, down below, and there is my beloved mushroom, and there is the Queen – she is arguing with roses that are every shade of the rainbow.

'I'll be back!' I call down, and they look up, and they get smaller and smaller

and smaller . . .

'When I've had an Adventure!'

About the Authors

Peter Bunzl is the author of *Cogheart*, which has won numerous regional awards, was selected as a Waterstone's Children's Book of the Month, nominated for the Waterstones Children's Book Prize, the Branford Boase Award and the Carnegie medal. The third book in the Cogheart series, *Skycircus*, is out now.

Pamela Butchart's bestselling Baby Aliens books include *The Spy Who Loved School Dinners*, which won the Blue Peter Best Book Award 2015, and *My Teacher is a Vampire Rat*, which won the Children's Book Award 2016. She has also written two brand-new Secret Seven stories, and a number of picture books. Pamela lives in Dundee with her family.

Maz Evans's debut children's novel, *Who Let the Gods Out* was selected for Waterstones Children's Book of the Month, has sold to seventeen countries worldwide, was shortlisted for the Waterstones Children's Book Prize, the Books are My Bag Readers' Awards and longlisted for the Branford Boase Award. Maz is the founder of Story Stew, a schools' creative-writing programme, and Book Buddy, a book donation programme for schools.

Swapna Haddow is the author of the Dave Pigeon books, shortlisted for the Sainsbury's Children's Book Awards, selected for the Tom Fletcher Book Club and winner of a number of regional awards. She is also the author of several picture books, including *Little Rabbit's Big Surprise*, and the forthcoming *My Dad is a Grizzly Bear*. She lives in New Zealand with her family.

Patrice Lawrence is an award-winning writer, whose debut YA novel, *Orangeboy*, won the YA Book Prize, the Waterstones Prize for Older Children, and was shortlisted for the Costa Children's Book Award. She is also the author of *Orangeboy* and *Indigo Donut*, as well as the 2019 World Book Day title, *Snap*.

Chris Smith is an award-winning journalist and broadcaster, having presented Radio 1's *Newsbeat* to millions of listeners daily, as well as hosting shows on BBC Radio 5 Live. He is the the co-author of the bestselling Kid Normal series with Greg James, which debuted in 2017 and was shortlisted for the Waterstones Children's Book Prize and the British Book Awards.

Robin Stevens grew up in California and now lives in Oxford. She is the author of the bestselling detective mystery series, Murder Most Unladylike, which won the Waterstones Children's Book Prize in 2015, and has been translated into eleven different languages. She is also the author of *The Guggenheim Mystery*, a sequel to Siobhan Dowd's *London Eye Mystery*.

Lauren St John worked as a veterinary nurse and a sports and music journalist before turning to children's books. Her bestselling White Giraffe series is inspired by her childhood in Zimbabwe, and *Dead Man's Cove*, the first in the Laura Marlin detective series, won the Blue Peter Book Award. Her new detective series, the Wolfe and Lamb Mysteries, began with *Kat Wolfe Investigates*.

Lisa Thompson's debut novel, *Goldfish Boy*, was selected as Waterstones Children's Book of the Month, nominated for the Carnegie Medal, the Branford Boase Award and the Waterstones Children's Book Prize, and sold in nine languages. She is also the author of *The Light Jar* and *The Day I was Erased*. She lives in Suffolk with her family.

Piers Torday's books include *The Last Wild*, shortlisted for the Waterstones Children's Book Prize, *The Dark Wild*, winner of the Guardian Children's Fiction Prize, *There May Be a Castle* and *The Lost Magician*, which won the Teach Book Primary Award 2019. He is also the writer of the stage adaptation for John Masefield's *Box of Delights*.

Amy Wilson is the author of *A Girl Called Owl*, which was a top-ten fiction debut, longlisted for the Branford Boase Award and nominated for the Carnegie Medal. Her other magical fantasy novels are *A Far Away Magic* and *Snowglobe*, which was selected for WHSmith Travel Book of the Month in December 2018. *Shadows of Winterspell*, her fourth novel, will publish in October 2019.

Discover Lewis Carroll's original classic stories

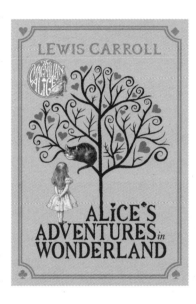

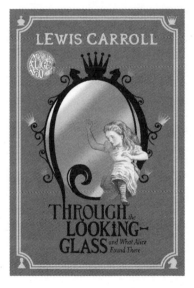

The perfect gift for all Alice fans

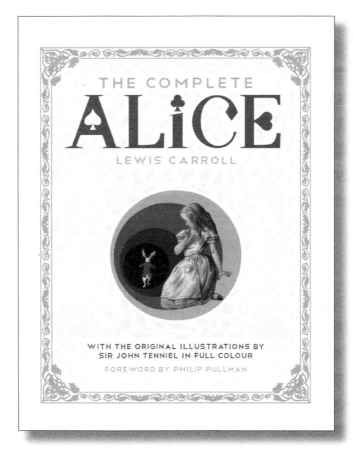